Bolan's c gone terr

He ran for the ne the underside of the armored... was still pouring a firestorm of destruction into the rooftops. While it raked the left side of the street, the townspeople on the opposite side tried to take the SUV out by concentrating their fire, but the lighter rifle shells ricocheted off the body.

Then Bolan heard an even louder racket above the earsplitting thunder of rifle fire as a shadow passed overhead. The helicopter came in low and out of the south, a pair of gunmen wielding M-16s shooting at the remaining riflemen on the roof. But then the M-249 on top of the Humvee swiveled and opened up as the helicopter approached, the 5.56 mm rounds spitting out to star the helicopter's windshield.

The pitch of the aircraft's engine changed suddenly, turning choppy. The helicopter's shadow began whirling around on the street as the pilot fought for control. Bolan watched the M-249 gunner pour more fire into the aircraft, and then heard a small explosion. The chopper reared up and accelerated right into a storefront, where its blades shattered into shards of deadly shrapnel flying in every direction. What was left of the fuselage crashed to the ground about fifteen yards from where Bolan was.

The engine of the Escalade started, and Bolan flattened himself against the ground as the vehicle lurched backward and he was left lying in the middle of the road, while the SUV barreled down Main Street.

Bolan was on his feet in a flash, running for the Humvee. The driver rolled down his window. "What's your plan?"

Bolan leaped into the rear of the vehicle and pulled back the cocking lever of the M-249. "We've got to stop them before they get back to the factory! They're going to blow it up!"

MACK BOLAN ®
The Executioner

The Executioner
Don Pendleton's
STAND DOWN

A GOLD EAGLE BOOK FROM
WORLDWIDE.

TORONTO • NEW YORK • LONDON
AMSTERDAM • PARIS • SYDNEY • HAMBURG
STOCKHOLM • ATHENS • TOKYO • MILAN
MADRID • WARSAW • BUDAPEST • AUCKLAND

Recycling programs
for this product may
not exist in your area.

First edition August 2011

ISBN-13: 978-0-373-64393-6

Special thanks and acknowledgment to
Travis Morgan for his contribution to this work.

STAND DOWN

Printed in U.S.A.

There is a certain enthusiasm in liberty, that makes human nature rise above itself, in acts of bravery and heroism.
—Alexander Hamilton
1755–1804

One takedown at a time, I will rid this world of the evil that threatens our liberty and way of life—that's not a threat, but a promise.
—Mack Bolan

THE
MACK BOLAN
LEGEND

Nothing less than a war could have fashioned the destiny of the man called Mack Bolan. Bolan earned the Executioner title in the jungle hell of Vietnam.

But this soldier also wore another name—Sergeant Mercy. He was so tagged because of the compassion he showed to wounded comrades-in-arms and Vietnamese civilians.

Mack Bolan's second tour of duty ended prematurely when he was given emergency leave to return home and bury his family, victims of the Mob. Then he declared a one-man war against the Mafia.

He confronted the Families head-on from coast to coast, and soon a hope of victory began to appear. But Bolan had broken society's every rule. That same society started gunning for this elusive warrior—to no avail.

So Bolan was offered amnesty to work within the system against terrorism. This time, as an employee of Uncle Sam, Bolan became Colonel John Phoenix. With a command center at Stony Man Farm in Virginia, he and his new allies—Able Team and Phoenix Force—waged relentless war on a new adversary: the KGB.

But when his one true love, April Rose, died at the hands of the Soviet terror machine, Bolan severed all ties with Establishment authority.

Now, after a lengthy lone-wolf struggle and much soul-searching, the Executioner has agreed to enter an "arm's-length" alliance with his government once more, reserving the right to pursue personal missions in his Everlasting War.

Prologue

Sandra Bitterman's carefully constructed world in Quincyville, Kansas, came crashing down around her on Thursday evening at 6:14 p.m.

Her husband Jack had called from the office, just like he did every night before coming home. Usually they talked of inconsequential things, but this night he seemed tense, distracted. He was speaking quietly, as if someone was nearby and he didn't want to be overheard.

Before she could ask him if anything was wrong, he said, "Oh, and about dinner, I've changed my mind. Don't put the roast in—we're going out."

Sandra had automatically started to reply before Jack's words registered. "Okay—what was that?" She'd heard what he'd said, of course, but for a moment her brain refused to process the words.

His voice took on that "don't-screw-around-just-do-as-I-say" tone she knew all too well. "I said, 'about dinner, I've changed my mind. Don't put the roast in—we're going out.'"

Sandra had always been quick on her feet, and now she leaped to the occasion. Still clutching the cordless phone to her ear, she walked across the Italian tile floor of their kitchen, past the thirty-six-inch gas cooktop, past the Brazilian wood cabinets and into the plush, cream-colored carpeted hallway. "Sounds good to me. Are we finally going to that steakhouse you've been dying to try?"

"It's a surprise. Just have Kelly ready to go. I'll be there soon. I love you, honey."

Sandra's heart hammered in her chest. She knew Jack loved her, but he rarely said it. That he'd chosen to say it at this moment told her just how serious things were. "I love you, too. We'll see you soon."

She backtracked to hang up the phone, then trotted to a cabinet above their glass door refrigerator-freezer and pulled the door open. Reaching in, she withdrew a compact Smith & Wesson Model 386 Night Guard chambered in .357 Magnum. Opening the cylinder, she checked the load, then flipped it closed again. She checked her pockets, but the slacks she wore wouldn't allow her to carry the pistol comfortably. Opening the maple bread box, she slipped the pistol inside, then ran upstairs.

Electro-pop music blared behind her daughter's closed bedroom room. Sandra didn't bother to knock, but twisted the knob and shoved it open, the door snagging on piles of dirty clothes. The room was a teenage explosion of angst and emerging style, with pop star and movie posters covering the walls. Her daughter lay on the bed, a textbook open in front of her. A tiny MP3 sound system pumped out the tunes as Sandra strode into the room.

"Mo-om, what the he—?" Kelly looked up from her algebra textbook with annoyance and reached over to turn off the player, but Sandra caught her wrist before she could. The expression on her mother's face cut her daughter off in midsentence.

Sandra put her lips close to Kelly's ear. "We have to go—now."

Kelly's mouth hung open as she stared at her mother. "You serious?"

"Damn right I am." When her daughter stared up at her, unmoving, Sandra clapped her hands. "Now! Move it!"

Rolling off the bed, Kelly ran for her walk-in closet, scattering clothes as she went. Sandra didn't wait to check her progress, but headed for the master bedroom, muttering under her breath. "Goddamn it, Jack, you told us they would never find out."

Sandra hadn't always been the upstanding pillar of the community she was now. She had grown up in an even more hardscrabble town—really just a gas station, church, small grocery store and two bars—named Malin, in the middle of nowhere in western Kansas. As soon as her feet had hit the ground, she was determined to get out before she became another faceless farmer's wife. She had dreams of escaping to the big city—Los Angeles, not Kansas City—but before she could do that, she met junior Jack Bitterman at Quincyville High School. A half-dozen dates, a six-pack and two joints later, she learned she was pregnant with Jack's baby.

Kansas being Kansas, marriage was the only realistic option. But Jack had surprised her—he had no plans to sit around and get a crappy job in Quincyville. Instead, he'd studied hard and graduated law school at the state university. The years of college had been rough on both of them, but when it was done, he'd sprung another surprise on her—they weren't going to the East or West Coast, but back to Quincyville to set up his practice.

When she'd complained about it, he'd asked her, "Listen, do you just want to be another lawyer's wife in New York or L.A., trying to raise Kelly in a cookie-cutter crap neighborhood while I'm putting in ninety-hour workweeks as a faceless junior exec in a huge firm, or do you want to be someone in a town where being the wife of an attorney will mean something?"

While she pondered that, he leaned closer and whispered.

"And don't you want to stick it to all those folks back home who said you'd never amount to anything?"

That had been all it took. And the past several years had been amazing. Although some folks had whispered about Jack's various dealings, it had turned out that he had a true gift for the law—and when and how it might be skirted when necessary. That talent had proved invaluable when the Cristobal Pharmaceutical Company had come calling.

By then Quincyville was dying, its younger generation fleeing the small town for greener pastures. Cristobal had wanted a small town in the Midwest to set up their base of operations, and Quincyville had been the logical choice. That was mostly thanks to Jack's behind-the-scenes dealings, greasing the wheels of local and county administrations, as well as the state legislature to push through a staggering package of economic incentives and tax breaks that made any other place in the state a fool's choice. And the men running Cristobal were no fools.

Lately there had been talk of Jack running for mayor—being responsible for the revitalized town, he would have been a shoo-in. And from there, who knew what could be next. State Senate? Governor? U.S. Senator?

But just a few minutes ago, Jack had spoken the code words that told Sandra it was all about to blow up in their faces. Running to her own walk-in closet, Sandra headed straight for the back, where a large, packed suitcase stood in a corner. Grabbing it, she hauled it through the bedroom and into the hallway, where her daughter stood, earbuds dangling around her neck, with her hand on a similar suitcase.

"Where's Dad?"

Sandra took the lead to the stairs. "He's on his way, but if he isn't here in ten minutes, we're taking the Escalade and will meet up with him later."

"Are we leaving because of something he did?"

Sandra shot a quick look at her daughter, but Kelly's expression revealed curiosity, not anger or disappointment. "I don't know, honey." She actually had a pretty good idea, though. The only thing that would scare him enough to leave town would be if the company had uncovered his skimming, although he'd sworn they would never notice. *"There's so much money flowing through there, they'll never realize a few grand is missing here and there,"* he'd said when he had first brought up the idea to her.

"Well, apparently they did notice, you ass," Sandra muttered. By the time they'd had that conversation, she'd figured out the real product the company produced, and had decided her husband was right. Still, she'd insisted they have an escape route ready to go, and had drilled it into her husband and daughter until they had accepted the reality, and could execute it in their sleep.

Hauling the heavy suitcase downstairs, Sandra wheeled it through the kitchen and into the attached garage, where she threw it into the back of the gleaming black Escalade that Jack had given her for their sixteenth wedding anniversary. He'd paid for it in cash, which probably wasn't a good idea, given how everyone in town knew everyone else's business. Probably attracted too much damn attention from one of the big shots at the company or something, she thought.

After hoisting Kelly's suitcase into the cargo area, she slammed the back door closed, then hit the button that would open the garage door. It crept up with agonizing slowness, and what it revealed outside made Sandra's heart leap into her throat.

Standing in the bright glare of the security lights was a slim man dressed in a sheriff's uniform, complete with a fur-collared jacket to ward off the prairie chill. He regarded her with a flat stare, his Hispanic features half-shadowed by his flat-brimmed hat. The nightstick on his right hip and holstered SIG-Sauer P-229 on his left hip contrasted with his relaxed stance.

Sandra stared at the man, trying to make her voice work. "Deputy Quintanar, what are you doing here?"

"Good evening, Mrs. Bitterman. I'm actually looking for your husband. I was just about to knock on your front door when I heard the garage door opening. I was wondering if we could go inside and talk." His voice was perfectly polite, but even in the glare of the lights, Sandra sensed his eyes—their cold, flat, reptilian stare—pinning her to the wall. Almost as if he knew what she was doing, and had caught her in the act.

Sandra sensed rather than saw Kelly frozen in the doorway to the house. Slipping one hand behind her back, she waved her daughter back inside while plastering what she hoped was a guileless smile on her face. "Of course, please come in. I'm afraid Jack isn't home yet. Would you like some coffee while you wait?"

The deputy smiled, looking anything but pleased. "That would be fine." He strode quickly into the garage. Sandra was already stepping back into the kitchen, whispering, "Hide!" at her daughter, who took off through the kitchen.

Sandra made a beeline for the bread box. Just as she was about to open it, she heard the deputy's voice from the doorway.

"I thought you were making coffee, Mrs. Bitterman."

She looked over to see him standing there, seemingly relaxed—except for his left hand resting on the butt of his pistol. Sandra smiled again. "Of course, but I have to begin preparing dinner as well."

"I wouldn't be concerned about that right now." Deputy Quintanar stepped into the kitchen and closed the door behind him. Despite his relatively small stature, his menacing presence dominated the room.

Sandra's heart tripled its beat, but she gritted her teeth behind her lips and motioned to a chair while she crossed to the coffeemaker. "Won't you sit down?"

"Thank you." He moved to a chair and pulled it out, but didn't sit. Sandra steeled herself and turned her back to him as she filled the coffeepot with water and poured it into the Braun machine.

"Regular or decaf?"

"Whatever you prefer is fine. Do you expect Mr. Bitterman to arrive soon?"

Sandra measured coffee beans into the grinder. "It's hard to say. He's been putting in a lot of late nights at the plant recently."

"So he has."

Cursing inwardly, Sandra hit the grind button. Would the deputy take that as a hint that Jack was up to something at the plant? Once the beans were reduced to a fine grind, she dumped them into the permanent brass filter, closed the brewing chamber and turned on the machine. The coffeemaker gurgled quietly as it worked. With nothing else to do, she walked to the refrigerator and opened it. "I hope you don't mind if I begin preparations while we wait for Jack."

Rustling about among the shelves, she heard the chair creak behind her. "I thought Jack was taking you and your daughter—Kelly, isn't it?—out to dinner this evening."

Son of a bitch—they were listening, she thought. Grabbing a ceramic dish of the previous night's beef stew, Sandra straightened, and closed the refrigerator door. "Why would you say that, Deputy?"

"You know how it is in big companies. Nothing is ever really private."

Damn. As soon as the words hit her ears, Sandra realized they knew everything. Her priorities shifted from escaping with Jack to making sure her daughter and she survived the next few minutes. Still holding the cold dish in her hands, she walked to the stove and twisted the knob to heat the oven, then opened the door and set the casserole dish inside, slipping the glass cover off as she rose. "I don't know what you mean by that—"

Putting everything she had into it, she whirled and threw the glass cover at where she expected the deputy to be. The moment she turned, she saw her error—he'd already stepped to the right, closer to the front door. The heavy glass cover sailed past his chest and slammed into the wall, gouging a chunk of drywall out before falling to shatter on the tile floor.

The motion had still caught the deputy by surprise, and he flinched from the breaking glass. Sandra didn't stop to see what he was doing, but lunged for the bread box, shoving the cover open and grabbing the revolver. Whirling again, she aimed the pistol at Deputy Quintanar at the same time he raised his own gun.

Even in the large kitchen with its high ceiling, the twin reports of the pistols sounded like claps of thunder going off right next to her. As she saw the deputy go down, Sandra also felt an impact on her upper chest, and immediately her right arm refused to work. She managed to get the gun into her left hand and edged around the kitchen table, conscious of the ringing in her ears and the trickle of warm blood dripping down her breast to pool in her bra. Spying a booted foot, she crept closer, pistol at the ready to finish off the deputy. His torso came into view, and finally his arms and head. Taking aim, Sandra was just about to squeeze the trigger when she caught a motion out of the corner of her eye.

Keeping the gun trained on the motionless body, she glanced over to see Kelly in the doorway to the hall, her mouth open in shock at what she was seeing.

"Kelly, get back, *now!*" Sandra bore down on the trigger, but the moment's distraction was enough. When she returned her attention to the prone gunman, Sandra saw he was pointing his SIG-Sauer at her, and fired.

The bullet plowed through her midsection, mangling her

large intestine and shattering her spine before punching a grape-sized hole in her lower back as it exited. There was a remarkable lack of pain; instead, it felt as if a large part of her body was suddenly just not there.

With all control of her legs gone, Sandra stayed upright just long enough to pull the trigger of her own pistol, the bullet flying harmlessly wide, before collapsing on the floor, landing hard enough to make stars swim before her. Her vision cleared enough to see Kelly coming toward her. With a tremendous effort, Sandra shook her head, mouthing, "Run…" Tears streaming down her face, her daughter vanished up the stairs.

Hearing movement from the other end of the kitchen, Sandra managed to twist her head back to see the deputy climb to his feet, breathing hard, but apparently none the worse for wear. She saw the hole in her jacket where her bullet had entered—a perfect heart shot—but Deputy Quintanar moved like he hadn't been shot at all. Bastard was wearing a vest…she thought.

He kept his pistol trained on her as he stepped forward. Sandra tried to raise her gun, wanting one more chance at the man who was about to take everything from her, but her numb arm refused to obey the command. Then he was next to her, nudging the revolver out of her hand and placing it on the counter.

"Although I admire your courage, Mrs. Bitterman, it is a pity you didn't choose to cooperate. Now your husband will have to see you in this state, to say nothing of your daughter. I'm sure he will cooperate fully with our investigation once he knows we have Kelly in custody."

He moved to step past her, but was stopped by her hand on his ankle. Although she already found it hard to breathe, she forced the words out. "You leave…my daughter…out of this."

He shook her off like a horse shook off a bothersome fly.

"I'm afraid that is no longer possible. You can be consoled, however, by the fact that you will not be alive to see what will happen to her."

Sandra steeled herself for the final bullet, but instead the deputy stepped past her and walked into the hallway, pistol in front of him as he searched the rest of the house.

Sandra felt herself growing cold, and realized that she was bleeding to death. She hoped Kelly had been smart enough to get out of the house—there were a few ways to leave, even from the second story. She knew the plan, but it had all counted on her securing a vehicle. On foot, she might make it to safety, but there were no guarantees. Sandra racked her brain. There had to be a way to enable her daughter to get to the garage....

The comforting smell of freshly brewed coffee wafted to her nose, and Sandra realized what she could do. She reached for the nearest cabinet, grabbing the stainless-steel handles, pulling each drawer out, and pulling herself up by them with her single good arm. Her injured shoulder throbbed with pain each time she moved, but strangely, she felt nothing below her waist, just numbness. The floor was slick with blood—her blood—making it easier to move, but she didn't know if she'd be able to stand up in the slippery pool. With all of her remaining strength, she twisted her body so she was facing the counter, and smiled as she saw her target just within reach.

She had just gotten her fingers on the pot handle when she heard noise coming from two different directions—the tread of the deputy's feet on the stairs, and the rattle of Jack's key in the front door lock. Twisting back again, Sandra opened her mouth to shout a warning, but simply breathing was an effort, to say nothing of trying to force air out to warn him off.

"Sandra? Sandra, where are you—oh my God!" Jack rushed in, skidding to a stop as he saw his wife slumped against the cabinets in a large pool of blood. "Jesus Christ—" He fumbled for his cell phone as she tried to form words while nodding toward the hallway.

For fuck's sake, she thought. He isn't paying attention... again...

"Mr. Bitterman, so glad you could join us." Sandra watched as Deputy Quintanar's words made Jack freeze with the cell phone at his ear. For a moment, he was oblivious to the pistol in the other man's hand, then he recovered his poise and pointed at Sandra.

"Why the hell are you just standing there? My wife's been shot! Help her, for God's sake!" Jack stared at the deputy while waiting for his call to connect. Deputy Quintanar didn't move a muscle toward Sandra, but turned toward Jack, his pistol more visible now.

"What are you doing?"

"We've noticed several discrepancies in the month-end statements—amounts not matching up in various accounts, that sort of thing. We've traced the discrepancies to your department. You are going to return with me to company head-quarters to answer some questions Mr. De Cavallos would like to ask you."

Jack's eyes widened as he realized what the deputy was there for. Sandra rolled her own eyes in disgust. Dumb bas-tard not only gets himself in trouble, but just makes it worse, she thought. With the last of her strength, she heaved the decanter of hot coffee at the deputy's crotch.

The scalding liquid splashed over his pants, making him shout in pain. Jack seized the distraction to leap for the pistol on the counter. Sandra heard a flurry of shots explode around her as her senses dimmed, her vision fading to black, her last memory the scent of Kona Blend coffee mingling with the coppery smell of blood all over her formerly spotless kitchen floor.

1

Damn, that horizon just keeps moving away, no matter how fast I drive toward it, Mack Bolan thought as he stared out at the endless prairie surrounding him on all sides. The gently rolling grassland was split only by the concrete ribbon of Interstate 70, stretching into infinity both in front of him to the east and behind him to the west. Occasionally the stark landscape would be broken up by a truck stop or restaurant near an exit, but for the most part there was nothing but Bolan, his car and the plains.

He smiled grimly as he considered the apt metaphor of the horizon, always retreating, endlessly out of reach. A lesser man would consider his personal crusade against the enemies of freedom in much the same way—always struggling to reach an ever-elusive goal. Bolan took a more pragmatic view of his ultimate objective. As he'd once said, "Every terrorist I kill, every madman I eliminate, every criminal I put in the ground, that's one less psychotic thug in the world menacing innocent people. If the job takes the rest of my life, then that's what it will take."

His commitment to his crusade against the enemies of freedom and liberty notwithstanding, after his last mission on the West Coast, Bolan, aka the Executioner, decided to take a few days of downtime and drive back to his base of operations, Stony Man Farm in Virginia. Although he was aware of several hot spots that could use his special kind of attention, he also knew constant combat took its toll on any warrior. The trip east had seemed to be a perfect solution at first. He'd planned to relax by driving the entire way, but after a half day of the endless Midwest grasslands, he was beginning to regret his decision. That was the problem with the prairie—absolutely nothing happened or changed out here. Maybe he'd drop the car off in Kansas City or Chicago and hop an airplane.

At least his rental car was comfortable. The slate-gray Cadillac SRX crossover rode across the asphalt as if he were driving a cloud. Bolan was half worried he might fall asleep if something didn't change soon.

Then something did happen—the low gas light turned on with a polite chime, almost as if the car were too polite to draw his attention to its condition. Bolan eyed the dashboard, then hit the GPS for the next gas station, locating one just a few miles away. Pulling in a few minutes later, he glanced around the barren refueling station, which had one other car in the parking lot. He filled the tank, and saw the sign as he was walking to the cinder-block building to pay.

Visit Quincyville
The Best Little Town in the Midwest!

Unlike most of the road signs out here, the red, white and blue board was as fresh and new as if it had been put up yesterday. Bolan stared at it for a moment, then headed inside.

Even though it was early spring, the air-conditioning was on full blast inside the store. Bolan paid his bill in cash, then nodded at the sign, still visible through the window. "Where's Quincyville?"

The clerk, a clean-cut teenager, pointed east along the

highway. "Just head down another mile, take exit 27, turn left and go about five miles up."

"A little slice of Midwest America, huh?"

The kid frowned. "If you say so. They wouldn't even be there if it wasn't for that bug pharmaceutical company on the outskirts. Saved the whole place from dryin' up and blowin' away."

"Is that so? Any place good to eat there?"

"Rollins's Restaurant on Main Street has the best chicken-fried steak in the county. Hobo stew's good, too."

Bolan considered it, his stomach chiming in to add its emptiness to the internal discussion. "Thanks for the tip."

"You're welcome, and have a good day."

Bolan nodded as he headed out into the warm afternoon. Getting back in his car, he got on the highway and followed the kid's directions. Less than ten minutes later, he saw a picture-perfect small town on the horizon. As he approached, Bolan noticed a cluster of several large, white buildings on his right. The complex was at the end of a double lane paved road with a manned guard shack at the end. The perimeter around the buildings was ringed with an eight-foot cyclone fence topped with double rows of razor wire. Between the road and the fence was a sign that read Cristobal Pharmaceutical Company.

Bolan's eyebrows rose in surprise at the sight. Typically, U.S. drug companies outsourced their labs overseas, not the other way around. Still, if they were making it work…

Cresting a hill, he saw a lone mansion in the distance on his left, with two police cars out front and yellow crime scene tape around the house. Bolan slowed the Cadillac and casually studied the scene as he passed, then shook his head as he headed into town. Seemed nowhere was picture-perfect anymore.

Passing a Walmart with a packed parking lot, he drove up Main Street, which was neat and clean in a way he hadn't seen in a long time. Pickups and midsize sedans filled the parking spaces, along with a scattering of luxury cars here and there. People were out and about, but they were few and far between, all intent on their business. Bolan passed the usual buildings—drug store, local grocery store, freestanding department store, more gas stations, various fast-food restaurants.

He found the Rollins place at the north end of town, an unassuming clapboard building that looked like it had been built in the 1950s. The parking lot was also filled, which Bolan took as a good sign. He found a spot on the end, almost in the weeds, and got out, glancing at the back seat to make sure his black duffel bag hadn't shifted during the trip. Satisfied that it was secure, he locked up the Caddy and headed toward the front doors.

The interior might have come right out of the 1950s as well. Near the door, the cash register sat at one end of the long Formica counter, with a row of stools, each covered with a patron. Booths with red vinyl seats ran along the wall nearest the parking lot, ending in a large corner booth filled with a boisterous group of teenagers laughing and talking to and over one another. The booths continued along the back wall, and in the middle of it all was a row of tables, also filled to capacity. Unlike many of the retro places that only appeared authentic, this restaurant was the real deal. The chrome edging the counter and booths looked well-used, but also well cared for, and the linoleum on the floor was faded and scuffed with the passage of thousands of shoes and boots.

Bolan entered into a bustle of activity: waitresses carrying trays piled-high with food, diners entering and leaving, and above all, that welcome smell of delicious, home-cooked food. The soldier caught the traditional aromas of cooking oil, bread and spices, but also sniffed what smelled like burning mesquite wood, which made his mouth water.

He dutifully took his place at the end of the line and waited his turn.

The conversation level in the place was muted, and Bolan noticed that many men and women kept their heads down, and at least once he thought he saw a woman come out of the washroom with red, mascara-streaked eyes. Although there seemed to be a lot of regulars, with headgear on the men split evenly between Stetsons and gimme caps, there were also plenty of people who had just come to eat, and the stools turned over quickly. Bolan was able to take a seat after just a few minutes.

"Coffee?"

"That'd be fine." Bolan scanned the menu, which had a decided Tex-Mex flair that caught him by surprise. Although the *carne asada* tacos looked good, he decided to stick with the kid's recommendation. "Chicken-fried steak, please."

"Gravy on your potatoes, too?" the middle-aged waitress asked.

Bolan glanced down at his taut midsection and decided to double-down on his arteries. "Sure."

"Green beans, salad, or a cup of soup?"

"Beans will be fine."

"That'll be up in a few minutes."

"Thank you." Bolan sipped his coffee, served in a thick-walled ceramic mug he hadn't seen in years, and found it very good. For a few seconds, he relaxed in the anonymity of the moment—just another casual traveler grabbing lunch on his way to wherever. His reality couldn't have been more different.

He was giving the rotating dessert carousel a twice over, debating whether to have the cherry pie or the apple tart afterward, when the low conversations throughout the restaurant suddenly died. Bolan looked over to see what was causing the disturbance and saw a group of four well-dressed Hispanics, accompanied by a lone Anglo girl, cut to the front of the line and saunter into the restaurant. They were dressed in formfitting jeans, hand-tooled, silver-edged cowboy boots, and soft, shapeless, button-down designer shirts, with expensive sunglasses covering their eyes or perched on their heads. Their short black hair shone in the overhead lights. The eyes of the locals either followed the group or looked away. No one made a move to stop them.

Not even glancing at the line of waiting customers, the group headed toward the large corner booth, where the kids there scrambled to get out of the way. Their leader stood in front of the booth, staring over his glasses at the dirty dishes left in the group's wake. Dead silence filled the restaurant, punctuated by the sizzle of grease on the grill and the tap-tap-tap of the young man's foot on the floor.

The busboy scurried out and cleared the table, but apparently not fast enough. Although Bolan couldn't see exactly what happened, he saw the boy carrying the plastic container of dishes stagger and go down with a crash of breaking dishes. His gaze darkened.

The group sat down, and conversation began around them again, even quieter now. Bolan looked up to catch his waitress staring daggers at the corner booth. "Who're they?"

She glanced at him and blushed. "Don't mind me. The one struttin' around like he owns the place is Everado De Cavallos." She drew the name out in a derisive drawl. "The other ones are his flunkies, a cousin and other friends from south of the border. He's the son of one of the big shots at Cristobal, so he thinks this town owes him whatever he wants. Plus he never leaves a damn tip either."

"Hmm." Bolan sipped his coffee again, then turned his head just enough to watch the group out of the corner of his eye. They were huddled together, awaiting their drinks, apparently, which were just arriving. The waitress set the glasses down and turned to go, but not before one of the boys on the end smacked her behind. A man with iron-gray hair in a bristle cut who was watching started to rise from his chair, but was restrained by his lunch companion, a woman with curly red hair, who shook her head. Still glowering at the group, the man sat down again, staring hard at the young men, who just as studiously ignored him.

That's two, Bolan thought, easing back on his stool as he kept an eye on the table.

"He does that again, he'll have me to deal with, Cristobal or no Cristobal," the waitress, whose name tag read Elaine, grumbled.

"Those boys might learn their lesson sooner than you think," Bolan said. The comment earned an odd look from the counter waitress before the cook called, "Order up!"

His blue-plate special arrived, and Bolan dug in, finding it as good as promised. As he ate, he kept an eye on the corner booth, waiting for them to act up again. But when it happened, it came from within the group itself.

"Goddamn it, Everado, I said knock it the hell off!" The shout was punctuated by the crack of a hand on skin. The next thing Bolan knew, the blonde girl burst from the booth and stalked off. The boys stayed behind for a few seconds, then their leader stood up and walked out, followed by the rest of the group, all of whom were still sniggering. Halfway through, he turned and glared at them, and the laughter died in their throats. They walked out to a gleaming midnight blue Mercedes-Benz convertible, where the girl was waiting with her arms crossed.

Bolan forked up another bite of his steak and turned to see the conversation get heated, with the girl and the guy both starting to gesticulate. She seemed unaware of the potential danger she was in, with the other boys starting to crowd around the couple.

That's three, Bolan thought, tossing a twenty-dollar bill on the counter and heading for the door. Once outside, he didn't even have to look over to see which way the argument was heading.

"—damn it, Everado, you don't paw me in public like I'm some piece of meat. I'm not one of those Mexican whores you can just fuck and forget!"

"*Chica,* just get in the car and we'll go somewhere quiet and talk about this," the young man said. He sounded reasonable, but his voice was pitched low.

"Fuck you, just take me home!"

Bolan shook his head. This girl really didn't realize the fire she was playing with. He'd heard that kind of tone in a man's voice more times than he cared to count. Ninety-nine times out of a hundred, violence was sure to follow.

Sure enough, the young man's hand came up, the girl's expression turning from anger to incredulousness to fear in a second. Bolan gave it a one-count, then said, "Hey." He'd pitched his voice at the exact same timbre, just loud enough to carry to the youth's ears, but not to attract any attention outside the six of them.

Everado's hand froze, and he whirled, as did his friends, everyone staring at the interloper.

"Where I come from, any man who's worth a damn doesn't hit women. It's not very—" Bolan paused, as if searching for the right word "—macho."

The leader looked at Bolan as if the older man had just walked up and slapped him. Everado took a step forward, his boots crunching on the gravel. "Is that right?" His cohorts fell in behind him as their leader approached the Executioner.

Bolan nodded curtly.

"You aren't from around here, are you, amigo?" The young man stopped a few feet away from Bolan, his posse fanning out around them.

Bolan stood casually and confidently, hands at his sides, his eyes on the leader. He knew the others wouldn't make a move unless Everado did first. They all thought they had the advantage with their numbers. It would take less time to show than tell them just how wrong they were.

Bolan shook his head slowly.

"Did you have a good meal in there?"

"I did, before it got interrupted," Bolan stated.

"Hey, no one asked you to stick your nose in, asshole!" This came from the girl, who was slouched against the convertible, apparently annoyed at not being the center of attention anymore.

Bolan and Everado ignored her. The young man took out a thick roll of bills and peeled off a fifty, tucking it into the soldier's shirt pocket. "Here's a little advice. Walk back inside, finish your lunch, order two more, I don't care. Then come back out, get into your car and keep on driving. That way nothing *bad* will happen to you."

Bolan had to work hard at suppressing his smile. Normally he'd give anyone who got in his face a bit of credit, but this kid was already in way over his head; he just didn't know it yet. "That wouldn't be a threat, now, would it?"

The young man smiled broadly and shook his head. "Not at all, man! But the prairie out here—so desolate. Travelers who are unprepared can lose their bearings pretty quickly."

"I'll keep that in mind." Bolan looked beyond him to the girl. "She isn't going with you, by the way."

The young man had started to turn back to his car when Bolan spoke. He froze again. "What did you say?"

"You heard me. She isn't going anywhere with you."

Everado turned back. "And I suppose you think she's going somewhere with you."

"Nope. She's staying right out here, in public, until one of her parents comes and gets her. I'll be nearby, just to make sure nothing *bad* happens."

This time the young Mexican got right up into Bolan's face, so close he could smell the well-dressed punk's cologne—a pungent, sharp fragrance. "You got a hell of a lot of nerve to come into our town and start givin' orders. Do you have any idea who I am?"

Bolan didn't back down an inch. "I sure do."

His confident answer caught the youth by surprise, and Bolan kept going. "You're a kid from south of the border who got lucky. Your grandparents scratched out a living in Mexico, so your parents wised up and joined Cristobal for a way out. You've never known a hard day in your life. You've never worked twelve, fourteen, sixteen hour days, only to eat, sleep and get up to do the same thing again, six days a week. You grew up with a spoon—not a silver one, just a regular one—in your mouth, so you've never had to do anything hard in your life, ever. You've assumed a status that you've done nothing to earn, and wear it like you have the right. But anyone who looks at you for more than two seconds sees straight through that. They can see right to your soul, see the aimless, ambitionless kid driving a fancy car and wearing designer clothes, and walking around like he knows what's going on. What those people really see is a boy who has absolutely no idea of who he is, where he came from, or what he's doing with his life."

Bolan leaned in close to the youth's ear, speaking so only he could hear his next words. "And deep down, I think you also know that—and it scares the hell out of you."

Much like his girlfriend's face a few minutes ago, Everado's expression changed from surprise to incredulousness to anger at hearing Bolan's assessment. "Fuckin' asshole!" He reached for Bolan's shirt, while the other young men crowded around them, hands reaching out to snare the interloper, as well. Bolan was a moment away from breaking fingers and moving on from there when the whoop of an approaching police siren made everyone's heads turn.

2

As soon as the rest of the young men heard the siren, they pulled away from Bolan, leaving him none the worse for wear. He noticed Everado's expression turn dark at seeing the car, and the young man muttered a curse under his breath.

The approaching sheriff's cruiser came to a stop in the parking lot, and a Hispanic deputy got out of the car. Bolan eyed the newcomer warily. Even with his mirrored aviator shades on, he resembled the youth close enough to be a relation, which meant the situation could turn bad really fast. The man slung a nightstick into the holder at his side, then took his flat-brimmed hat from the seat beside him and put it on before walking over.

He nodded at Bolan. "Sir." Then he turned his attention to Everado and the rest of his boys, all of whom were looking anywhere but at the two men. "Everado, what's going on here?"

The young man stared at Bolan for a moment, then looked away to spit on the ground. "Nothing—sir."

"Got an anonymous tip of a fight going down in the parking lot at Rollins's place. Now you boys wouldn't know anything about that, would you?"

The group all muttered negative replies.

The deputy turned to Bolan. "Sir, was there any sort of alter-cation here that you'd like to report?"

Everado spoke up then, "But, Rojas—"

The deputy turned his mirrored sunglasses on the young man, causing his words to die in his throat. He turned back to Bolan. "Sir, you are?"

"Matt Cooper."

The deputy didn't write it down, but Bolan was more than willing to bet he'd made a note of it. "Again, did anything go on here that you would care to report?"

"No, thanks. I just thought I saw a misunderstanding, and had come out to see if there was anything I could do to help."

"That what happened, Everado?"

The young man had turned from hard case to indignant to sullen in the span of a minute. He nodded. "Yeah."

"All right, then. Glad to know you boys aren't causing trouble." The deputy leaned over to spot the girl against the convertible. "Connie? I'm sure school isn't over till the end of the month."

The girl rolled her eyes and stared off into the distance.

The deputy's voice turned steel-hard. "Come over here, girl."

She stared at him, then slowly walked over. Everado's mouth opened as if he was about to say something, but the deputy turned his gaze back on the young man, and he shut it with a snap.

Connie stood in front of him. "What?"

The man nodded toward his cruiser. "Get in. I'll take you back to school."

Like her boyfriend, Connie was about to try to argue, but the lithe deputy's stance made it clear he wouldn't be having any of it. "Goddamn it," she muttered as she stamped around the cruiser to the passenger side and got in, slamming the door closed.

The deputy turned to the group of young men. "And I better not get any more reports with any of your names in them, else I'm coming after all of you, you hear? Now you all get gone."

Casting resentful looks back at Bolan, who had just stood and watched the whole affair, the youths got into the Mercedes-Benz. Everado started the car and backed out, then drove sedately off.

Deputy Quintanar—Bolan caught his name tag as he turned—watched until the youths were out of sight, then turned back to Bolan. "On behalf of the rest of the folks here in Quincyville, I'd like to apologize for what happened. They're what passes for the resident hell-raisers around here, and have to be reined in now and again."

Bolan nodded. "Boys will be boys, and all that."

Quintanar cocked his head. "No, not quite. I imagine his father will be talking with him about this very soon. You know how small towns are—nothing's ever really private."

"I guess so."

"Hope you enjoy the rest of your time here." The deputy turned to go back to his car.

"Oh, Deputy…" Bolan waited until the man had turned half around before continuing. "It's probably none of my business, but I noticed the large house on the hill with the police tape around it. I'm kind of an amateur crime buff. Can you tell me what happened over there?"

Deputy Quintanar stared at him for a few seconds before walking back over. "I hope you won't misunderstand my response, Mr. Cooper, but you're right—it is none of your business. However, if you must know, one of our most prominent citizens and his wife were shot and killed last night. We're going to find whoever did it, don't you worry. Now, why don't you go back inside and enjoy the rest of your meal?"

"Suppose I'll do just that. Thanks." Bolan walked back to the diner door and turned to watch the cruiser pull away.

Walking back inside, he was surprised to be greeted by a smattering of applause, started by Elaine behind the counter, then spreading throughout the place. Bolan noticed several men who didn't join in the accolade, either glaring at him or averting their gaze altogether. He understood how they felt—although he wasn't sure whether they were jealous of it or embarrassed that they hadn't stepped up—but he wasn't thrilled with the reception, either. Waving a hand halfheart-edly at everyone, he went to his stool and waved Elaine over. "Thought I might finish my lunch."

"Damn straight you will—on the house. Luke, another blue-plate special!" A few minutes later a heaping plate filled with enough food to choke a grizzly bear appeared in front of him. Bolan eyed the platter, then looked up at Elaine, who stared at him expectantly. "Dig in, honey."

"I'll try." Bolan did just that. The stares and whispers didn't take the edge off his appetite, and he made a good dent in the double portion of everything before calling it a day. Slipping the fifty out of his pocket, he tucked it under the plate, but before he could remove his hand, the waitress cleared her throat.

"I said your meal was on the house."

Bolan flashed her an easy smile. "And I thank you, it was delicious. This tip is from Everado and his boys. Make sure the busboy and their waitress get their share, will you?"

Elaine's mouth dropped at the denomination before she swept it into her pocket. "I most certainly will. You stop by here any time."

"I will, thanks." Bolan walked out into the afternoon sun and looked down the street, half expecting to see the punks in their convertible lying in wait for him as he left the park-ing lot. He looked around at all of the clean, neat buildings and people going about their business. Everything seemed normal.

Maybe that was it—everything seemed almost *too* normal.

Bolan checked his watch. If he was going to hit Chicago today, he should have already been on the road. Still…

He got into his rental vehicle and pulled out his smartphone, running a quick internet search to find the information he was looking for. Starting the Caddy, he drove to the main intersection of town, then turned right and drove another half mile before pulling into the parking lot of the *Quincyville Gazette*.

Getting out, he walked past a vending machine with the latest issue in it—the cover story was about the latest round of crop subsidies being voted on in the state legislature. Stepping through the front door of the A-frame building, Bolan walked up to a long counter with a plump, young, bottle-blonde woman behind it. "Can I help you?"

"Yes, I was wondering if you had your back issues on computer file or microfilm?"

"The library would be more likely to help you with those kinds of records. May I ask what you're looking for?"

"Sure, my name's Matt Cooper, I'm a freelance stringer for the *Capitol Journal*. I'd heard there was a double homicide here in town recently, and decided to come out and see if I could get the story."

While he talked, the receptionist's face went from curiosity to confusion to concern. "Would you wait here for a moment? I'm going to get someone to help you."

"All right." Bolan cooled his heels in the reception area for less than a minute. The receptionist hustled back out with an attractive brunette woman in her mid- to late-thirties.

"This is the gentleman I told you about."

The older woman held out her hand. "Casey Hinder, editor-in-chief."

Bolan introduced himself again using the Cooper alias. "Perhaps there's somewhere we can talk more privately?"

"Absolutely, why don't you come back into my office?" She led him behind the counter, past a cluster of fabric-walled cubicles, some empty, others occupied by employees. At the back of the large room was a row of offices. Casey ushered Bolan into the corner one, which was slightly larger than the others.

"Have a seat." Bolan did so while Casey closed the door and crossed around the back of the desk, sitting in an old wooden-backed chair. "Okay, buddy, who the hell are you really?"

Bolan frowned. "I told you, I'm—"

She held up her hands. "Save it, there's no way you're a stringer for the *Topeka CJ*. Mainly because this 'story' hasn't even gone out over the wire, so there's no way you're from that paper, as they don't even know about it yet. Then I get a call about a dark-haired man resembling your general description who goes toe-to-toe with Everado De Cavallos this afternoon and walks away in one piece."

Bolan smiled. "Deputy Quintanar had something to do with that."

The journalist shook her head. "Whatever. Look, my source—who knows what they're talking about—says it looked like you were about to mop the floor with them. I may be the editor-in-chief, but I had my share of bylines before I reached this desk, and it doesn't take much to figure this one out."

"I don't think your source saw the same conversation I had with Everado." Bolan leaned back in his chair. "All right, I'll level with you. I'm a freelance journalist on my way back from a convention in Las Vegas. I stopped in for lunch at the diner, heard about the double homicide and thought I might be able to get a story out of it."

Casey's slim eyebrow rose. "A freelance journalist?"

Bolan nodded.

"Driving a brand-new Cadillac?"

"Rental. You wouldn't believe how many frequent flyer points I've racked up on my credit cards."

"Pardon my bluntness, but you look way too fit to be a stringer."

Bolan smiled again. "Thanks for noticing—I try to keep fit."

His implication hit the editor after a moment, and she colored slightly. "Hmph." She studied him for a long minute. Bolan returned her frank, green-eyed gaze with his own pair of vibrant blues, not saying a word. "You got some kind of press pass, online clippings, website, anything?"

Bolan shook his head. "Not anything recent. Website got hacked by the Chinese in retaliation for a piece I did on the tongs last year. Even I can't access it without getting spammed with a thousand pop-ups for 'enhancement' products. Even passed out all my business cards in Vegas."

"Yes, how convenient." Casey rested her elbows on the desk. "All right, I'll give you what I know, on one condition—you give me twenty-four hours to break the story first, all right?"

"Sure, I'd have to sell it first anyway, so no problem."

Blinking in surprise at having won so easily, Casey recovered and leaned back in her chair. "The decedents are Jack and Sandra Bitterman. Jack was basically the town lawyer. He handled just about everyone's business here. He also was the main factor behind Cristobal locating their first North American laboratory here. Once they arrived, he served as legal counsel for the company in its dealings with the township."

"Yeah, I've been researching them since I got here. Seems like an unusual place to locate a state-of-the-art facility, don't you think?"

Casey had slipped on a pair of tortoiseshell glasses and regarded Bolan over the rims. "That question's been asked many times before, and the heads of the facility say they wanted a place where it was peaceful and quiet. No doubt the tax break package Jack lined up with the state government had something to do with it as well."

Bolan had been doing an internet search again, and held up his smart-phone. "This victims?" He'd located a picture of the family, a man, woman and teenage girl, who looking to be about seventeen years old, posing at some kind of county fair next to a blue-ribbon science project.

"Yeah, that's Sandra, Jack and Kelly..." Casey's voice trailed off.

Bolan asked the obvious question. "Where is the daughter now?"

Casey stared at him as if he'd just sprouted wings. "Oh my God, just fire me already... The sheriff's department hasn't mentioned a single word about her yet."

"So she's still out there somewhere, yet from what you just said, the sheriff hasn't put out an Amber Alert for a missing teenager, or sent out any sort of BOLO announcement yet."

Casey's expression had gone from disgust for not seeing the connection to uncomfortable at Bolan's comments. Before she could reply, her desk phone rang. "Excuse me, will you?"

She picked up the phone. "Hinder, editor's desk...yes, Principal, how can I help you?...she was where?...Yes...I'll be right over to discuss it with you...thank you."

She slammed down the phone, then looked up with haunted eyes. "Do you have any children, Mr. Cooper?"

Bolan shook his head. "Haven't found the right opportunity yet."

"Well, if you ever decide to take that particular plunge, think long and hard about it before you do—they're equal parts heaven and hell, but my daughter seems to be leaning toward the latter recently."

"Let me guess—she was caught skipping school and brought there by a Deputy Quintanar, right?"

Casey had been rising from her chair while Bolan talked, but stopped halfway to the door, her mouth open. "How'd you know that?"

"She was at the diner when I ran into Everado. Matter of fact, she was with Everado—"

Casey cut Bolan off before he could finish. "Goddamn it all to hell! I told her to stay away from him! Nothing good's gonna come from her hangin' out with any of them. Sorry to cut this short, but I gotta go." She handed him a card. "If you need anything else, you know where to find me."

"That I do. Thanks for your assistance, and good luck with your daughter." Bolan rose and got the door for Casey.

"I'll need more than luck to deal with her today." They both walked into the bullpen to see Deputy Quintanar talking with the receptionist. He looked up to see Casey and Bolan together, and his brow furrowed in puzzlement before he smoothed his expression over while waiting for them to approach.

"Ms. Hinder, I was wondering if you had a few minutes."

"Sorry, Rojas, but I got a problem I have to take care of first. Maybe we can catch up later this afternoon?"

"That would be fine. I'll check in with you later." He kept an eye on Bolan as Casey ran out of the building. "You're certainly taking an interest in our little town, Mr. Cooper."

Bolan nodded. "I've been looking for a place to settle down for the past few months, somewhere quiet, peaceful. I thought Quincyville might be just the town I've been looking for. I was asking Ms. Hinder about local businesses that might be hiring and properties available for rent or sale."

The deputy digested this story for a moment. "Quincyville is always glad to have new folks settle down here. It's a good place to raise a family. What line of work are you in?"

In for a penny, in for a pound, Bolan thought. "Private security. I used to work for Blackwater, but got out before the government stuck its nose in too far. Times have been a bit tight lately. That's why I was looking into local businesses. Right now I'm into whoever can give me a steady paycheck."

His reply seemed to relax the deputy somewhat. "Interesting. If you do decide to call Quincyville home, perhaps you and I should talk again. It's possible I could recommend you to our company as a security specialist."

Bolan frowned. "Our company? I thought you worked for the state?"

Quintanar's frown matched his for a second, then he smiled. "That's true, but all of us here in Quincyville are very proud of what Cristobal has done for the town. I hope you'll excuse our possessiveness."

Bolan nodded with what he hoped looked like relief. "Doesn't matter much to me, as long as the pay's steady. Any word you could put in would be great, although I wouldn't expect you to have much trouble out here."

"You'd be surprised. There are always problems that need attention in the pharmaceutical business—corporate espionage, product transfer security, even bodyguarding our senior officials when they travel outside the U.S. A man with the right experience could prove to be very useful."

"I'd appreciate the opportunity to talk with your superiors if possible. Truth be told, except for that Caddy outside, my pockets are a bit on the light side at the moment. If I decide to stick around, I'll be in touch."

The deputy tipped his hat. "Hope you do. I'll see you around." He pushed the door open, holding it for Bolan to follow him out, then headed for his cruiser. Bolan watched him leave before getting into his own car and hitting the speed-dial for Stony Man Farm.

"Hey, Striker, looks like I win my bet with Hal." The cheerful voice of Aaron "the Bear" Kurtzman sounded in his ear. "I knew you wouldn't be able to go more than twelve hours before checking in."

"I was thinking the same thing about you guys," Bolan said dryly.

"So how's the road trip going?"

"Funny you should ask. I've run into a bit of a detour in a town called Quincyville, in Kansas."

"What's going on out there?"

"I'm not quite sure yet. If you're only tackling the usual three or four things at the moment, can you check the national law-enforcement databases for information on a double homicide involving an attorney named Jack Bitterman?"

"He the vic?"

"Yeah, apparently he and his wife were both killed some-time yesterday."

"Okay, just a sec." Bolan heard Kurtzman's fingers flying over his keyboard. Stony Man Farm intelligence-gathering apparatus was unrivaled by any other organization in the world, and Kurtzman was the brains behind making it all work. After a few seconds, the analyst spoke up. "I got noth-ing on local, state or regional DBs. No bulletins or anything. You didn't have anything to do with this, did you?"

"No, but the local sheriff's department is keeping it on the QT, which seems really strange. Do me a favor and have Akira place a cover file for Matt Cooper setting him up as an ex-field employee of Blackwater, let go in the recent past under questionable circumstances. Tag any inquiries origi-nating from Quincyville ISPs and trace them back to their source host."

"We're on it. You looking for a good or bad jacket?"

"Make it gray—charges brought but nothing proved. Prioritize that one. I have a feeling someone's going to be checking out my background very quickly. That reminds me, 'Matt Cooper's' last mission was as a DOJ agent. Delete that file. I don't want this guy stumbling across that jacket while searching for my other fake identity. If anyone needs to check my DOJ affiliation, I'll have them make a call."

"I'm on it. Anything else?"

"Yeah, do a search on cell phone records for a Kelly Bitterman. That's their daughter, who's been missing since yesterday, and hasn't been found yet. Two more things. First, get me a jacket on a deputy out here named Quintanar." Bolan spelled the name as he recalled it from the deputy's nameplate. "First name Rojas."

Kurtzman's fingers sounded like they were moving so fast, Bolan could have sworn he smelled plastic melting. "Got it. What's the second?"

"There's a company in town named Cristobal Pharmaceuticals. They seem to be a big player here. What can you tell me about them?"

Bolan heard more tapping. "I can send you their most recent quarterly statement if you'd like. Let's see… Founded in 1987 in Veracruz. Originally known as a health-food company, selling herbal supplements and the like. Bought out in 2004 by Cristobal Enterprises out of Maracaibo, Venezuela, which renamed itself the Cristobal Pharmaceutical Company. They built their U.S. headquarters in 2006 in Quincyville, Kansas. No initial ties to criminal organizations that I can find, however, it seems Cristobal, no matter how it's been reinvented, has a rather tangled past. It's been passed around several South American holding companies like a hot potato. Want me to keep digging?"

"Absolutely. And let me know when you've accessed Kelly's phone records. I want to know if she's contacted anyone in the past twelve hours."

"You got it. Hey, if Hal calls for you, what should I tell him?"

Bolan's mouth quirked up in a half smile. "Tell him I'm doing a little house hunting in Kansas."

3

Deputy Rojas Quintanar didn't waste any time calling his superiors once he left Matt Cooper at the newspaper. But he wasn't reporting in to the sheriff. Instead, he speed-dialed a number that connected him to the Cristobal complex.

"De Cavallos."

"This is Rojas. We may have a problem." He quickly outlined the confrontation with Everado outside the restaurant, and his subsequent conversation with Matt Cooper at the Gazette building. "If this guy is who he claims to be, it's pretty coincidental that an ex-PMC guy just happened to wander into our town for lunch."

"What's your take on him?"

"Definitely ex-military—he's got the bearing. He may be who he says he is, but he could be government too, possibly trying to insert as deep cover. He seemed pretty interested in finding work, so perhaps we can reel him in that way, and take care of him on our turf if necessary."

"I'll run a check on him, see what comes up. Find out where he's staying and make sure someone's keeping tabs on him," De Cavallos said.

"All right. Also, please keep Everado from doing anything loco. We don't need him attracting any more attention than he already has."

"You concentrate on doing your job, Rojas, and let me worry about my son, understand? How are you doing finding the girl?"

"We've been combing the entire town and are watching the house—"

"Wait a minute, you think she'd actually go back to the homestead where her parents died?"

"We're covering all the bases, just in case. We're also monitoring her friends' homes and their cells in case she contacts anyone, but so far she hasn't popped up anywhere."

"Damn it, you need to find her, and quick. If she saw anything last night and talks to anyone, you're screwed."

"Don't worry about it. The second she appears, we'll be all over her."

"You better be. I'd hate to have to lose such a good deputy over this."

Quintanar swallowed hard. He knew De Cavallos didn't mean he'd be facing criminal charges. If he was lucky, he'd end up in a shallow grave somewhere on the prairie. If De Cavallos was really pissed, there was always the microwave oven… The deputy shuddered at the thought. "Like I said, we're on it. Besides, where's she gonna go?"

"Who knows? She's a kid who just saw her parents get killed. Did you check on other family?"

Quintanar frowned, letting a bit of annoyance creep into his tone. "Of course. She's got grandparents in Lincoln, Oregon, but she hasn't contacted them yet. If she does, we'll triangulate the call and go get her."

"Let's hope that's exactly what happens. You let me know the moment you have a lead on her. And be sure to tell those brothers of yours that I want her alive. We'll need to know she hadn't told anyone anything before we take care of her."

"Yes, Mr. De Cavallos." Quintanar disconnected the call, resisting the urge to slam the cell phone against the steering wheel. That girl was the only loose end in what had been a perfectly planned operation, and every hour she was missing was more time that she could be talking to someone about what she had seen. They had searched the house thoroughly, but found no trace of her. Maybe one of her friends might be able to get in touch with her. Hell, maybe one of her friends could get her to come out of hiding, he thought.

Pulling back onto the road, he dialed Everado's cell. "*Hola,* Everado. Yeah, well…if you hadn't been acting so macho, I wouldn't have had to shut you down like that. But I got a way for you to get out of this little mess with your old man…I'll tell you, if you just shut up and listen for a minute…"

CASEY TRIED TO KEEP her anger in check as she drove toward the newspaper building again. Glancing over at her daughter, she found Connie staring out the window, tinny music playing through the earbuds attached to her brand-new iPod Touch, which Casey hadn't bought, and Connie didn't have the money for. At a stop sign, she reached out and yanked the left one from the girl's ear.

"What is your problem?" Connie turned to glare at her mother, snatching the bud out of her hand.

"What the hell do you think is my problem? Skipping school to hang out with that Everado boy? Are you out of your mind? Do you have any idea how dangerous that is?"

Connie rolled her eyes. "Gee, Mom, since you never tell me anything, no, I don't have any idea. Why is seeing him dangerous? Is it because he's a Mexican?"

"No, that's not it, but…" Casey stopped, wanting to tell her daughter of her suspicions about Cristobal, but knowing she couldn't risk it. There was no way Connie would keep her mouth shut about it, and then they would be as dead as the rest of the town would be if the word ever got back to the heads of the company that someone was talking.

Instead, she took the opposite tack. "Look, honey, I'm just concerned about you. Everado's from a wealthy family—"

"Yeah, and we're poor white trash. Thanks for reminding me." Connie crossed her arms and stared out the window again.

Well, at least she included me in that assessment, Casey thought. "No, dear, that's not what I was saying at all. I'm just worried that he might consider you a—" with no delicate way to say it, she plunged ahead "—just a way to pass the time here."

Connie's head whipped toward her again. "Is that what you think—that I'm just some *norteamericano* slut to him?"

"Absolutely not—"

"You're damn right! Everado loves me. He told me so himself!"

Oh great, just what I want to trust—the word of a spoiled young man one step away from the drug trade, Casey thought. "All right, dear, I hear you, and no doubt he believes that as well—"

"Of course he believes that, why wouldn't he? I can't believe I'm hearing this!" Connie looked like she was about to jump out of the battered Ford Bronco at the next light. Casey reached over and put her hand over her daughter's— not grabbing it, but simply getting her attention.

"Sweetheart, listen to me. You and I have had this talk before, the time when Peter left, remember?"

Her daughter's face twisted in anger and hurt for a moment, then she smoothed over her pretty face and nodded.

"And you remember what we told each other—that neither of us would lose sight of who we are for a man—*any* man. I just want you to keep that in mind, okay? You may find this hard to believe, but I know a thing or two about love, and what it can do." Casey ignored her daughter's eye roll and kept talking. "And I know how hard it is to keep in mind what's real and what's not."

Peter sure did a damn good job of blurring that line, she thought. "I want you to keep your eyes open in this relationship, okay?"

Connie shook her head. "Don't worry, Mom. I know what I'm doing. Everado is like any other guy—more concerned with his macho reputation than anything else. But I *know* he really cares for me, and I care about him too."

Oh, the certainty of the young, Casey mused, resisting shaking her head. The only thing to do now was to accept her daughter's pronouncement as sincerely as she could. "Of course you do, honey. I didn't mean to imply otherwise. I just want you to be careful in what you do with him. Can you promise me that?"

Connie looked at her mother like Casey had just sprouted another head. "You aren't going to do a reprise of the 'birds and bees' speech, are you?"

Casey grinned. "No, once was enough. I trust that you're smart to take the appropriate precautions. But you're still in trouble for skipping school."

"Aw, Mom…"

"No buts, young lady. I will not have you slinging hash here or working a checkout counter at the local dollar store because you didn't finish high school. You are graduating, and you are getting out of here and going to college."

Casey felt Connie's stare on her. "And what if Everado said no?"

Casey inhaled, then lobbed the question back at her daughter. "What if he did?"

Her daughter shook her head, blond hair gleaming in the sun. "There isn't a man alive who's gonna tell me I'm not going to college."

"That's my girl—but you're still grounded for two weeks."

"What? Oh, come on, Mom—"

"One more word outta you and it's a month."

Connie opened her mouth, then realized silence was the better part of valor and closed it again.

"All right. Look, I gotta head back to the office and finish up the work that I was interrupted in the middle of by the call to get you. You get started on your homework, and we'll grab a pizza on the way home."

"Mmm. Mexican from Rollins's, with extra sour cream?"

"Sure, dear." Casey let out her breath, pleased to have navigated that conversational minefield with her daughter. They were just within sight of the newspaper building when Connie's cell phone rang.

"Hello?...hey, Everado...I know, I know, don't worry about it...we'll talk later...really?" She cupped her hand over the mouthpiece. "He says Deputy Quintanar wants to talk to me about the Bittermans."

A cold ball of ice coalesced in Casey's stomach. "What about?"

"I don't know—hold on." She put the phone back to her ear. "Why?...Well, yeah, I knew her, but not well...she was kinda stuck up, if you know what I mean—all right, all right, if he's there, I expect we'll talk to him...okay...bye." She flipped the two-year old clamshell phone closed. "The deputy thinks I might be able to reach Kelly on her cell if I call her."

"I thought you told Everado that you didn't know her that well."

Connie shrugged. "We were on the forensics team together for a year, so she knows of me. I can get her number. Hey, maybe I could say that you want to talk to her, get her side of the story."

A small ray of hope bloomed in Connie's stomach next to the ice. As much as she didn't want her daughter involved in the "investigation," if the deputy was going to officially request Connie's assistance, and Casey could gain something by it anyway, then there was no reason not to try and turn lemons into lemonade.

"We'll see, dear. Let's keep that idea between you and me for the time being." Casey spotted Quintanar's cruiser parked outside the *Gazette* building. "Let's see exactly what the deputy wants, and we'll go from there, okay?"

JACK BITTERMAN AWOKE to find himself duct-taped to a chair in an empty, rectangular, metal-walled room, still dressed in the light blue button-down shirt and black slacks he'd left the office in to go home and get his family the night before. His shoulder and arm throbbed unmercifully, and he glanced over to see a large, drying bloodstain running down his shirt. The lower legs of his pants were stiff and crusted, and as the memory of the past few hours crashed down upon him, he realized that his clothes were sticky with his dead wife's blood.

He didn't have time to reflect or grieve about it, however, because the large metal doors at the end of the room opened to reveal three men—two outfitted in security uniforms and carrying three tires, and the third one dressed in a charcoal-gray suit. The two men took up positions on either side of Jack and set down the tires. The suited man stepped forward into the light.

Jack glared at him with all the rage he could muster. "Mr. De Cavallos, what is going on? Why am I being restrained? Why did a sheriff's deputy come to my fucking house and kill my wife?"

The suited man walked over to Jack and took his face by the chin, lifting it up to the light. Jack blinked back tears as the naked bulb shone down on him. "Jack, Jack, Jack. Please, don't embarrass either of us with this pretense of not knowing why you're here. We know everything you've been doing over the past several months—the skimming, the copying of internal documents so you could cut a deal either with us or the U.S. Attorney's Office, all of it. Right now your home computer is being wiped of any incriminating files, and we were going to let your wife and daughter go if they had cooperated—after all, you were the one who had betrayed us, not them—but when Sandra tried to kill Rojas yesterday, well, it was obvious that the corruption had spread deeper than we'd originally thought. We've taken care of your wife, and we have you here now. There is one more person, however, who may have details of what you were doing with our company—your daughter, Kelly."

Ignoring the pain that flared in his shoulder, Jack gritted his teeth and strained against his bonds. "You leave her out of this—she had no idea what was going on, goddamn you!"

De Cavallos spread his hands in a show of helplessness. "I wish I could believe that." He nodded at one of the men, who walked back out the door, while the other one produced a knife and began cutting Jack free. "Are you aware of something called the *microondas,* Jack?"

Trying to rub feeling back into his hands and feet, Jack shook his head. With his gaze on De Cavallos, he missed the other man take a tire and slip it over the lawyer's head.

"The term translates roughly as 'the microwave.' It originated in Brazil, Rio de Janeiro, actually, used as a punishment for people who cooperated with the police."

Another tire was slipped over Jack's head, resting on the first one, and covering him from his knees down. "What are you doing?"

"The suspected informant is made to stand in a tower of tires." A third tire went around Jack, then a fourth. At the same time, the second man returned, carrying a bright red container. "Then the entire stack is covered in gasoline and set on fire, burning the person alive."

A fifth tire went around Jack, concealing his waist. It was followed by a sixth tire. De Cavallos held up his hand at the seventh. "Tell me where your daughter may be hiding, and I will kill you quickly, you have my word. Tell me nothing, and my men will finish the job."

Jack looked at him for a long moment, inhaled as if he was about to speak, then spit in the man's face. "You may have taken my wife and destroyed my life, but I'll be damned if you're gonna take my daughter, too. Go to hell, you god-damn motherfucker."

De Cavallos took out a silk handkerchief and wiped his cheek, then nodded at his men to continue. "After you, Mr. Bitterman."

The tire tower continued until it completely covered the lawyer. The second man poured the entire two gallons of gasoline over the column, making Jack gasp and choke as the harsh liquid rained down on him. There might have been a brief, muffled sob from inside the rubber cylinder, but then the room fell silent again, the hush broken only by the drip of gasoline. De Cavallos hesitated, in case the other man might relent, but then he nodded to the first man, who lit a match and dropped in into the gas trail they had poured to the entrance.

The gas ignited, the fire racing to the soaked tires, which went up in a whoosh of flames. A single, long, agonized scream came from the inferno, then the tortured voice inside fell silent, and the only noise was the crackle of the inferno and the hiss and pop of melting rubber.

Closing the door to the modified cargo trailer, De Cavallos turned to his two security men. "Get all of the men together, on duty, off duty, I don't care. We're going to get that Bitterman *puta* and find out everything she knows."

4

It took Bolan less than an hour to set up a suitable base of operations. First, he found what had to be the last independent motel in the area, a single-story building where each room opened to the outside—just what he was looking for. He paid for two nights, then checked out the room, making sure the window in the bathroom opened easily and quietly.

Next he bought a local paper and scanned the small want-ads section until he found a house for rent on the outskirts of town. A quick call set up an appointment, and he drove out to look the place over. It was exactly what he needed—far enough away to be private, yet close enough that he could be on Main Street in five minutes if necessary. He toured the two-bedroom, one bathroom ranch house with detached garage in under two minutes, noting the water-stained ceiling, a moldy odor emanating from the bathroom, the back door leading into a nearby field, and came back out.

"It's perfect. Your ad said five hundred a month?"

The landlord, Arnold Tolliver, a skinny guy with glasses, an underbite and receding brown hair, sighed. "Yeah, and I can't really come down on the rent."

Bolan was already counting out hundred-dollar bills. "Not what I asked. Here's the first month and the security deposit." He held out the money, which the guy snatched up, his eyes wide. Bolan kept his hand out. "Keys?"

"Oh, yeah." Arnold nearly fumbled the keys getting them out of his pocket, but managed to hand them over. "Let me know if you need anything else."

"I will." Bolan waited until Tolliver had driven away before getting to work. Taking his black duffel bag inside, he opened it, took out three small wireless cameras, walked outside and placed them in hidden vantage points that gave him a view of the front and back of the house through his laptop. Walking back down the driveway, he set up an infrared motion detector that would alert him to any vehicle coming up the driveway.

Going back inside, he changed into a black turtleneck and black combat pants, exchanging his slip-on shoes for well-worn combat boots. Next he turned to his weapons, giving them a cursory yet thorough review to ensure that they were in top working order. By the time he was finished, the twilight was fading into night.

Bolan slipped his Beretta 93-R into a clamshell holster that he secured at the small of his back and pulled on a windbreaker over that. Zipping the bag, he tossed it into the back of the Caddy and drove back into town, heading through the main drag and out toward the way he had come in that morning. Passing the Bitterman house, he kept going, driving until he found the first side road heading west. Turning onto it, he drove for another mile, then pulled over to the side of the road.

Opening the bag again, he selected the equipment he'd need for the next few hours, then closed the bag, slammed the door and locked the vehicle. Night had fallen, and the sky was lit up with an array of stars that Bolan rarely saw. Not sparing the country landscape a second glance, he started walking back down the road.

Ten minutes later, he was close enough to spot the Bitterman house standing in dark relief against the sodium arc lights of the city. Deep ditches had been carved out on either side of the road to handle flash floods, although they were currently bone dry. Bolan descended into one that gave him a good view of the house and the surrounding area. Removing a small pair of night-vision binoculars from a side pants pocket, he activated them and scanned the house, the grounds and the fields on either side of the plot of ground, looking for any activity.

He stayed there for an hour, watching. He also noted the frequency of cars passing on the highway. There were six total. After spotting no activity around the home, he checked all around for any suspicious vehicles or people in the vicinity. Seeing none, he rose from the ditch and walked toward the back of the house. Once there, he paused just before walking onto the property and scanned for motion detector lights or any obvious security. Seeing none, he put his binoculars away, flipped down a fourth generation night-vision monocular over his right eye and moved to the back door, which opened onto a brick patio with a built-in barbecue grill.

He noted there was no crime-scene tape securing the door, then scanned it and the surrounding framework for any kind of cameras or security setup. Not finding any, he went to work on the door with his picks and had it open in less than ninety seconds. Easing the door open an inch, he extended the end of a small fiber-optic camera attached to a monitor and panned the room, making sure no one was waiting for him. Satisfied, he pushed the door open enough to slip inside, then closed and locked it behind him.

Bolan found himself in a large living room, with a giant flat-screen TV mounted on one wall, surrounded by a long, leather sectional couch, a couple of matching recliners and other assorted furniture, all illuminated in his monocular's green glow. To his right was a hallway with a stairway off it leading up to the second level. The hallway itself continued on into what appeared to be the kitchen. Bolan spared a quick look upstairs, but smelling familiar odors from the room ahead walked there instead.

The stink of spilled blood and burned cordite was still very noticeable in the air. Seeing large stains on the floor and cabinets, he flipped up his night-vision gear and took out a small flashlight to examine the dried blood. Carefully stepping around the evidence, he studied the scene from several angles, trying to figure out what exactly had gone down here. From the spray patterns, at least two people had been shot, but there were odd movement patterns in the pool, as if one of the victims had come in after the first one had been killed—or while they were being killed.

Shaking his head, Bolan switched off the light and resumed using his night vision. He scanned the rest of the kitchen, finding a few bullet holes in the cabinets—one in the southeast corner, a neat hole in the molding around the doorway a few inches off the hardwood floor, and two near the refrigerator, one having punched a neat hole through the stainless-steel side of the appliance. Someone was shooting at whoever was here, he surmised. Without a forensic workup, there was nothing more he could learn from this room.

Bolan moved through the rest of the first floor, finding nothing but regular living space. Heading back to the stairway, he crept up to the second-floor landing, listening for any signs of life. Scanning the bedrooms, he quickly found the master, which had an adjoining room that had been used as an office, complete with a computer. It was off, and Bolan switched it on, waiting for it to run through its warmup routines. When it was finished, he tried to access it but was blocked by a password request. The soldier was about to place a call to Kurtzman when he heard a faint noise from another room—the scrape of something, maybe a foot, against a wall.

Drawing his Beretta, he attached a stubby suppressor to the extended barrel and noiselessly walked toward where he'd heard the sound coming from—the girl's bedroom. Halting outside the door, he listened, waiting for any other sound. Trying to ease the door open, he grimaced as it caught on something, stopping before he could ease his way inside. Before he could try to clear it, he heard another noise—the clink of something on porcelain. Stepping back, he moved down the hall to the nearest bedroom, a neat guest room that had a good view of the hallway and the girl's doorway. Keeping his pistol at his side, Bolan stood just inside the door and waited.

He had to give whoever was inside credit—they weren't rushing to get out of the room. Long minutes passed, but Bolan was far too used to lying in wait to let someone else get by him. At last, the door slowly opened, and a teenage girl with bedraggled hair and a sweat-streaked face peeked out.

Bolan pulled back, not wanting to startle her back into hiding. He heard movement in the hallway beyond. Edging out just far enough to see around the wall, he saw her creeping toward the stairs. He was about to call out to her when the moonlight gleamed off something in her hands.

Kelly had a gun.

Bolan gritted his teeth. She was so wired now that any noise, any approach would most likely end up with him getting shot. There was only one way to play it, and he didn't hesitate.

Holstering the Beretta, he moved out into the hallway, grateful for the thick carpeting that muffled his footsteps. Kelly was still creeping toward the stairs, every sense alert for any sign of life. Bolan centered himself, raised his hands and walked directly at her.

She was so intent on what was ahead of her that she didn't hear the movement from behind until it was too late. When Bolan was a step away, her head raised, and she started to turn, but not soon enough.

Swiftly, he clamped one hand around her mouth, while his other hand grasped the frame of the revolver she was holding, making sure to get the fleshy part of his hand under the back of the hammer, so even if she did pull the trigger, it couldn't move back far enough to fire. Letting out a muffled squeal, she reflexively squeezed the trigger, but only made the hammer dig into the web of skin between Bolan's thumb and index finger. He didn't have the leverage to lift her off the ground, and he was rewarded for his efforts by a hard kick to his shin.

"Stop struggling, Kelly, I'm not going to hurt you!" he hissed into her ear. He had to repeat his words again, as she simply tried harder to escape. Twisting hard, he wrenched the pistol out of her hands, which freed her fingers to claw at his face. Bolan reared back, dropping the gun on the ground and wrapping his free arm around her upper chest, pinning one arm against her side. Her other hand scrabbled across his face, and he twisted away from her fingers, not wanting to risk getting scratched in the eye. Despite his weight and height advantage, both of which were considerable, she fought like a wildcat.

"Damn it, knock it off! I work for the Justice Department of the United States!" That seemed to get through, for she suddenly stopped struggling. "Listen to me very carefully. I know something strange is going on in this town, and from what I can tell, your parents were killed because of it. The only thing I can promise you right now is that you're much safer with me than anywhere else at the moment. Do you understand?"

A second passed, then the girl nodded slightly.

"All right, if I let you go, will you promise not to run? In return, I promise to do everything I can to help you."

Another nod, quicker this time. "Okay, on three. One… two…three." Bolan took both of his hands away, and the girl whirled, tensing to flee, but watching him carefully. Her eyes flicked to the pistol a few feet away, then back to Bolan.

"Who the hell are you?"

Bolan slowly moved his left hand to his back pocket. "I'm Matt Cooper, Department of Justice, Domestic Security Section. I'm going to show you my badge, nice and slow, all right?"

She nodded, watching his hand as he brought out the wallet with its laminated ID card that confirmed what he had just said.

She didn't seem convinced, however. "What are you doing here? Who sent you?"

Putting his wallet away again, Bolan decided to take a gamble by telling her some of the truth. "I was heading back from the West Coast, and just stopped in your town for lunch. I heard about the shooting of your mom and dad, and what I found out didn't seem to add up—including the fact that no one seemed to know where you were—so I thought I'd check it out a bit. Seeing as I found you hiding in your own house, not with relatives or law enforcement, I'd say something's definitely going on, right?"

Kelly's lower lip trembled when Bolan had mentioned the death of her parents, but she managed to restrain herself, crossing her arms and hugging herself. "You have no clue how much shit I'm in, and probably you, too. I—I know who killed my mom and dad—I saw it happen."

Before Bolan could prod her further, he heard a click from below. He eased over to the stairway, but saw no lights come on. Nevertheless, his hunter's senses told him other people had just entered the house. "We've got company. Is there any way to leave the house from this level without being seen?"

"For me, maybe. I don't know about you."

"Then we're going out the back way." Drawing his Beretta again, Bolan scooped up the revolver and slipped it into his pocket.

Kelly frowned. "I don't get that back?"

"You ever shoot at another person before?" Bolan asked.

She hesitated, then shook her head.

"Then no, you don't get it back. Now be quiet and stay behind me."

5

Deputy Rojas Quintanar drove as fast as he could through town with his cruiser's lights off. The call had come in just as he had gone off shift, an automated message from the silent alarm alerting him that someone was moving around in the Bitterman house.

He'd wasted no time, calling De Cavallos immediately and letting him know what was going on. The other man's orders had been straight to the point. "Get that little bitch and bring her to me. I'll send over a few men, in case she puts up too much of a fight for you."

Biting back a retort, Quintanar had simply confirmed his orders and signed off. Next he'd called his brothers, Maximo and Silverio, and had them meet him at the end of the driveway to the Bitterman house.

By the time he'd gotten there, a black Escalade was also on-site, with three men standing around it. Quintanar grimaced at the sight, already regretting informing the head of Cristobal security about what he'd found. The other sheriff's cruiser, with the two Quintanar brothers inside, was parked a few yards away. He stopped his car, and all three got out at the same time, Rojas nodding to his brothers, the squat and solid Maximo, and slender and deadly Silverio. Both of the other deputies were carrying night-vision goggles, as well.

"It's just one girl—I don't think we're gonna need all of this to catch her."

One of the hired guns, a rail-thin Mexican dressed in all black with dusty cowboy boots, stared right through him. "Mr. De Cavallos said we are to assist in any way necessary."

Quintanar wasn't about to get into a pissing contest with them, so he simply nodded. "All right, but let us take the lead. Silverio, take these two—" he nodded at the other two gunmen "—and head around the back. Maximo, you and he are coming with me up driveway and through the front door."

Maximo reached into the second cruiser, coming back out with an Ithaca Model 37 Stakeout shotgun with a pistol grip. As he racked the slide, he caught Quintanar's glare and shrugged. "Just in case. After all, the mom almost got the drop on you. Who knows what other surprises they might have around the house?"

The deputy wished his older brother hadn't mentioned that in front of the Cristobal men—he didn't need it getting back to De Cavallos. With a sigh, he waved the others out. "We'll give you three minutes to circle around, then we're heading up. Do *not* kill her—De Cavallos said specifically to take her alive." He made sure each man heard him and confirmed his order with slight nods. "All right, get going."

The three men jogged off into the darkness. Rojas glanced at his watch, counting the seconds. When the allotted time had passed, he nodded toward the home in the distance. "Let's go."

The three men walked up the driveway. Quintanar was glad to see that the Cristobal shooter hadn't brought anything crazy like a submachine gun. He just carried a matte-black Glock in a belt holster. The deputy hoped the other two men would be just as professional—they didn't need this turning into any more of a potential public relations disaster than it already was.

Walking to the door, he produced a key and carefully inserted it into the front door, turning it as softly as he could. The click of the dead bolt unlocking still sounded loud to him.

"No lights." Turning on his night-vision monocular, Quintanar eased the door open and slipped inside, followed by his brother and the hired gun.

BERETTA AT THE READY, Bolan leaned over the banister, searching for any movement. The narrow hallway leading to the family room and the kitchen was a death trap, but so was staying upstairs. With no choice, he turned to Kelly.

"You're right behind me, got it? If we can't get out of the hallway, go back upstairs, and you're out one of the windows. If I tell you to run, you run, understand?"

She nodded, and he began creeping down the stairs. The night vision gave him an advantage, but only if the shooters didn't turn on the lights. He reached the landing without incident and paused, straining his hearing for any movement.

There! A boot heel clicked against the tile floor in the kitchen. They were already too far inside. He couldn't reach the back door in the family room without being seen.

Putting his back against the wall that abutted the hallway, Bolan waited, pressing Kelly against the drywall next to him. The man or men in the other room were good—they moved about with a minimum of signals or noise. But finally, one approached the hallway, paused outside, then peeked his night-vision-equipped head into the landing—and ended up staring into the muzzle of Bolan's Beretta.

The Executioner placed the sound suppressor right next to the man's temple. "Don't move," he whispered. "Step in here."

The gunman stepped through the doorway, the pistol in

his hand pointing toward the ceiling. Bolan quickly took it from him. He was dressed in a sheriff's deputy uniform, which made Kelly gasp when she saw him, recognizing the man a second before Bolan did.

"He killed my parents—fucking Rojas!"

She lunged forward, bumping Bolan's arm, making his pistol waver for a second. The deputy dropped his shoulder and bulled into the soldier, shoving his arm away as he pushed the other man as hard as he could. Instead of trying for the gun, he scrambled up and backed out into the hallway, shouting, "In here! Gun! Gun!"

"Damn it!" Bolan grabbed the back of Kelly's shirt and hauled her away from the doorway just as shots lit up the kitchen. Pushing the girl to the floor, he covered her with his own body as drywall erupted under the impact of several bullets.

"Stop, cease-fire, damn it!" a voice shouted from the other room. "Kelly, this is Deputy Quintanar. I'm here to help you. Tell Mr. Cooper to toss out his weapon and surrender, and we'll sort all of this out down at the station."

"Fuck you—" was all the teenager could get out before Bolan clapped a hand over her mouth.

"Deputy, this is Matt Cooper. I'm a special agent with the Department of Justice." As he spoke, Bolan pushed Kelly up the stairs, putting a finger to his lips and pointing to the second floor. She took the hint and began crawling up on her hands and knees. "I'm ordering you all to drop your weapons and stand down. Once I've ascertained that you pose no further threat, then I'll let you alone have your sidearm back."

As he'd figured, his demand caught the men outside off guard. There was a hurried conference, the men whispering in sibilant Spanish. Bolan's command of the language was good, but he was hard-pressed to keep up with the fast conversation, although he heard *mierda,* Spanish for "shit," more than once.

"Wait a minute," another man asked. "How do we know you're with Justice? I think this guy's just playing with us."

"I'll be happy to show you proper identification once I've secured all of you to my satisfaction. You can think whatever you want, tough guy, but if you take me out, I guarantee this place will look like the main plaza at Homeland Security headquarters in twenty-four hours. Now drop those guns and raise your hands!"

Bolan heard more whispering among the men. He knew there was almost no chance of them taking him up on his offer, but hoped the thought of tangling with the U.S. government might make them think twice.

"All right, Agent Cooper, we want to cooperate fully with the United States government. As a show of good faith, myself, my fellow deputy and the other man out here are going to slide our weapons over to you."

Bolan heard the sound of metal on tile and looked down to see the muzzle of a pistol in the entryway. Ducking, he pulled out his fiber-optic camera and extended the small lens around the corner, holding it high to give the illusion that he was still standing. No shots came through the wall. Bolan played the camera around the kitchen, seeing three men, all Hispanic, Quintanar and another one in sheriff's uniforms, and the third dressed all in black. All of them had their hands in the air. Bolan swiveled the camera down to verify that all three guns were on the floor, then checked out the rest of the dark hallway, but saw no one there. The real problem was what did he do with these three once he had them. One of his inviolate rules was that he didn't make war on officers of the law, but Kelly said this one had been the man who'd killed her parents, and Bolan couldn't stand dirty cops. But what if she was wrong?

"Both deputies, reach down slowly and take out your

handcuffs. Do it now." He watched as the two removed the metal bracelets from their belts. "The one on the left, cuff your left hand to the deputy's right, and the middle man do the same for the man next to him."

"What? Fuck you, man!" The man in black shouted. "You're probably the one who killed those people yesterday and have come back to finish the job! I'm not letting myself be cuffed just to get killed!"

"Goddamn it, shut up!" the first deputy ordered. "I'm afraid we cannot do that, Agent Cooper. We've demonstrated our trust in you, now it's time to show some in return. Come out and let's talk this over like civilized men."

Bolan withdrew the camera and appeared in the doorway just enough to point his Beretta at the middle man, giving him plenty of time to track and shoot the man on either side if necessary. "All right, I'm here. Now—"

The click from the darkened family room was all the warning Bolan needed. He pushed himself back into the stairway alcove as a shotgun boomed from only a few yards away. The pellets shattered the molding and wall, sending bits of it flying out in a spray that covered the stairs. Fortunately, the shooter had been so close that the pellets hadn't had time to spread, otherwise some of them might have tagged the soldier.

Bolan stuck out his Beretta and fired a 3-round burst into the kitchen, then one into the family room. Drawing his pistol back, he leaped up the stairs as fast as he could, hearing the shotgun's slide rack another shell into the chamber as he tried to put as much distance as he could between himself and the shotgunner. Another boom rocked the house, and more of the alcove below disintegrated as Bolan hit the second-floor landing on his hands and knees.

"Matt—" Kelly's voice sounded like it had been cut off, and he heard the sounds of a struggle from the master bedroom. The door was ajar but closed. Bolan decided to use the element of surprise and dropped back to his knees as he pushed the door open. A pistol blazed above his head, its muzzle-flash illuminating the shooter next to an open window on the far wall. Bolan tracked the man with his Beretta, and the weapon sit three rounds into his chest, the bullets pulverizing his breastbone and heart and making the attacker sag against the wall, a smoking gun dropping from dead fingers.

Hearing a muffled scream from outside, Bolan crab-walked to the wall next to the window and peeked outside without revealing himself, keeping an ear open for any gunmen coming up the stairs after him as well. The curtains were blowing, so he couldn't get a good look to see if anyone was waiting for him on the other side. Easing the tiny camera on its flexible extension around the corner of the window, the soldier spotted a dark form waiting to cap anyone who stuck his head outside. Bolan stuck his Beretta out the window and fired another 3-round burst, letting the pistol's recoil track the bullets upward. He heard a surprised grunt, then a groan of pain, followed by a thud as a body hit the roof.

Turning, he peeked out the window to see a crumpled body on the shingles, a pistol lying next to it. Bolan was climbing out the small window when he heard footsteps pound up the stairs. Drawing the revolver, he pointed it at the door and unloaded four shots. The footsteps stopped abruptly.

Bolan pocketed the revolver and exited to the roof, stopping only to grab the dead gunman's pistol. In the distance he saw another man in a deputy's jacket carrying a kicking, struggling Kelly down the driveway. Trotting to the edge, Bolan holstered his Beretta and placed the other gun on the roof next to him as he started to let himself down.

"Aquí!" A voice called from the window, and Bolan glanced up to see one of the deputies from the kitchen level-

ing a pistol at him. Grabbing the gun from the roof, Bolan snap-aimed a shot at him while jumping off the roof. He landed on the lawn, rolling with the impact and coming up in a crouch.

"He went around the side! Go, go, go!" Voices shouted from inside. Bolan ducked under the eave of the house, waiting to see if the deputy would be careless enough to peek over the side to try to find him. He was. The moon cast his shadow on the lawn, right above Bolan, and he pointed the captured pistol at the roof and fired three shots. There was a strangled yelp, then a loud thud, followed by a scream that split the night.

Bolan was already running into the darkness, shoulders tensed for those first few seconds as he expected a bullet to come from the house and tear into him, but after he was twenty yards away, he breathed a little easier. He redoubled his speed, trying to catch up with the deputy who taken Kelly. She was the only link he had to her parents' murder, and he'd be damned if he was going to let these thugs take her.

The driveway was long, but Bolan flipped down his night vision to see the man shoving Kelly into the back seat of a sheriff's cruiser, backhanding her across the jaw to take the fight out of her. Bolan gritted his teeth and unlimbered his Beretta, pulling up and taking aim. It was a long shot, but he'd made them before.

The 9 mm bullet whizzed through the air where the deputy's head had been just a second before. Drawing his pistol, he scrambled into the car, turning it on as he did so. Bolan shot again, his bullet shattering the side window, but the deputy already had the car in motion. But instead of speeding away, he cranked on the wheel and gunned the engine, sending the heavy vehicle straight at Bolan.

6

Bolan flipped up his monocle just in time to avoid being blinded by the cruiser's headlights. Instead of dodging out of the way, he leveled the Beretta and the captured pistol and unloaded both guns at the grille and front tires of the car, shattering one headlight and making sparks fly off the metal ram bar. At the last second, he dived aside, the car's rear tires spitting gravel over him as it passed.

Tossing the other pistol away, Bolan reloaded his Beretta and chambered a round. The shot-up cruiser kept going, but one of its tires suddenly flattened with a bang, and steam started coming out from under the hood as it coasted to a stop. The soldier ran toward it, pistol up as the deputy scrambled out, his own gun raised. Bolan fired high, his bullets shattering the red-and-blue lights on the car's roof, and forcing the deputy to duck behind the vehicle.

Reaching the other side, Bolan crouched behind the rear tire, flipped his night vision back down and glanced underneath, trying to spot the deputy's feet. Apparently the other man had the same idea, since Bolan couldn't see him no matter which way he looked. A loud thumping was coming from inside the car. Bolan had just decided to go to the front tire and use the engine as cover when the cruiser's rear window exploded into hundreds of fragments. The soldier glanced up to see Kelly crawling out of the back window.

"Stop right there!" the deputy shouted. Kelly slid down the trunk while Bolan stood up and shot through the open back windshield into the glass of the driver's window, making the deputy dive for cover again.

"Kelly, over here!" Bolan whispered. The girl scrambled toward him, and as soon as he could reach her, the soldier grabbed her arm and took off into the night. "Run as fast as you can for the ditch!"

The girl didn't need any urging, easily keeping up with Bolan and leaping into the dry ditch just as they heard the shotgun slide rack again and a boom erupt from the stalled cruiser.

"Go go, keep moving!" Bolan heard shouts from the house and the car, and knew the deputy and his men would be pursuing soon. He wished he'd gotten close enough to disable the other cars, but there hadn't been time.

"How far are we going?"

"Just past your property line, then cut left into the field." A few yards later Kelly popped up out of the ditch into a field of green timothy grass, already knee high. Bolan followed, glancing back on the run. The remaining gunmen were at the other two vehicles. He'd cut the force against them by half, but the remaining three men could easily run them down with the vehicles. Even as he watched, the SUV powered up, keeping its lights off as it pulled into the driveway, cutting across the lawn while the cruiser kept to the road.

"My car's about three-quarters of a mile from here, parked down the side road on the other side of your house." Bolan handed her the keys. "Think you can reach it?"

"Yeah, but what about you?"

"I'm going to divert them so you can get away. Stay hidden until I draw them off. Once you're gone, head for the

Miracle Mile Motel, park in back and wait for me in the car. Got it?"

Kelly nodded. "I'm not sure it's a good idea to split up—"

"We don't have a choice. Get to the other side of that hill, then run as fast as you can. Go!"

Bolan stood, presenting a clear target as he ran in the opposite direction. As he'd hoped, the SUV shot toward him immediately, its engine roaring. Bolan ran as hard as he could, trying to find any sort of cover to duck behind. Unfortunately, he had just entered a grassy field, and other than a few small hillocks, there was nothing else in the vicinity.

Gunfire sprayed from the SUV's windows, the bullets whining as they kicked up dirt around his feet. With no other options, he ran for the ditch again, using the berm for cover as the Escalade came closer. Stopping to check the load in his Beretta, he peeked up at the highway to see the sheriff's cruiser approaching, cutting off escape to that direction. The Escalade would be on him in a few seconds, unless…

Sticking the Beretta into its holster, Bolan dropped to his hands and knees and crawled as fast as he could down the ditch toward the Bitterman house. As he'd hoped, he found a small drainage pipe that went under the road. It was barely wide enough for his broad shoulders, but he didn't hesitate, wriggling inside as fast as he could. If they figured out where he'd gone and cut off both ends of the pipe, he was screwed, but Bolan still didn't waver, shinnying through the dry, dusty tube, aiming for the circle of green-lit darkness a few yards away.

He heard shouts from above, the men yelling at one another over where their quarry might have gone. Reaching the other end of the drainage pipe, Bolan quietly climbed out and snuck back down the ditch to the intersection south of the Bitterman home. He looked back to see the cruiser driving slowly along the ditch on the other side, but he couldn't see the SUV at all. Might have tried to catch up to Kelly, he thought. Making sure the deputy in the car couldn't see him, Bolan ran across the road and into the other ditch, then started up the side road back to his Caddy.

The growl of an engine to his right made Bolan turn his head. He saw the Escalade burst out from behind the house, juking and weaving, as if it was following someone running ahead of it. Bolan saw Kelly running with every ounce of strength she possessed, but still being cut off by the SUV every dozen yards or so, making her veer off in a different direction. Bolan's blood boiled at how the driver was toying with her. Glancing behind him to make sure the cruiser wasn't coming yet, the Executioner rose out of the ditch and loped toward the chase on an intercept course.

Finally, Kelly couldn't run any farther and made a last furtive attempt to slip around the SUV, which easily cut her off, coming close enough to smack her with the right front fender. She skidded to a stop on the ground, rolling over on her back, panting out clouds of vapor in the cool night air.

The Escalade stopped a few yards away, and a man got out of the driver's side, pointing a pistol at the girl. Kelly raised her hands. The man marched over, grabbed her by the arm and began hauling her back to the SUV. He'd holstered his pistol and was speaking into a cell phone as he reached the vehicle.

"Boss? Yeah, I got her. I'm bringing her back right—" was all he had time to say before Bolan stepped out from behind the SUV and put a bullet into the back of his head. The man dropped to the ground, his fingers sliding off Kelly's arm as she stood stunned for a moment before looking around wildly and seeing Bolan walking toward her. She sagged against the vehicle with relief, then froze as he put a finger to his lips.

The dead man's cell phone was still on, with a voice on

the other end saying, "Mateo? Mateo? What's happening? Where are you?"

Bolan picked up the cell. "Mateo can't come to the phone at the moment, and won't be able to ever again, seeing as how he just got a bullet between his eyes."

There was silence on the other end for a few seconds. "Is this the American? The ex-Blackwater employee?"

Bolan wasn't in the mood to play. "Nope. I'm your worst nightmare—a Department of Justice agent who just survived almost being killed by sheriff's deputies and men in your employ. I assume I'm speaking to someone at the Cristobal Pharmaceutical Company?"

"You are speaking to the head of security, in fact, Mr. Cooper. I don't know how or why you wound up in our little town, but I'm afraid you won't be leaving any time soon."

"You're right, I won't—not until I've burned your entire operation to the ground. I wouldn't worry about finding me anymore. I'll be coming after you now. You'll be seeing me very soon." Bolan snapped the phone closed and waved Kelly to the passenger side of the SUV. "Get in, we're taking this ride."

She ran around the hood and climbed into the seat. Bolan took a few moments to strip the man of his pistol and extra magazines, then got in and drove toward the road.

There was an unopened bottle of water in the cupholder between the seats. Bolan handed it to the teen. "All right, drink, and then tell me everything you know about what's going on here."

Kelly gulped long swallows before lowering the bottle. "I don't know all that much. My dad was involved with bringing Cristobal in from the beginning. He said it would revitalize Quincyville. Well, it has, but over the past couple years, the company's been exerting more and more control over what's been going on in town. They've got several people on the town board, the county, the chamber of commerce, you name it, they've got a hand in it."

She drank from the bottle again, almost draining it. The cell phone on Bolan's leg rang. He glanced down to see R. Quintanar in the caller ID box. Flipping the phone open, he closed it again as he turned right onto the highway heading south toward the interstate. "I'm sorry to have to ask this, but what happened to your parents?"

"I don't know! I know Dad was really busy working with the big shots at Cristobal to make sure everything ran smoothly. From what I could tell, they were planning to expand their operation to other regions, using the Quincyville plant as their distribution center. Apparently they've already got smaller shipping points established all over the country, but they want to decentralize more."

Bolan glanced over at her, his eyebrow raised. "How do you know all of this?"

"When there's nothing else to talk about over dinner, you end up listening instead..." Kelly's eyes welled with tears up as the impact of what she'd just said hit her.

Bolan checked his rearview mirror. As expected, he saw a familiar-looking sheriff's cruiser approaching fast. "Again, I'm sorry about what happened, but you have to tell me as much as you can." Off to his left, he saw the brightly lit grounds of the Cristobal factory. Instead of turning in, which he knew the deputies would expect him to do, Bolan pressed the gas pedal to the floorboard, making the SUV's big engine growl as it surged forward down the road.

Kelly glanced back. "Shit, I thought we lost these guys."

"Not yet. Keep talking."

"So last night my mom comes up to my room and tells me we have to leave, like right now. She was pretty practical about it, having a bag packed for each of us."

Bolan checked on the cruiser again, which was about fifty

yards away and closing. "Why'd she do that? Seems like you all had a pretty sweet setup there."

Kelly shrugged. "I don't know. About seven or eight months ago, she and Dad started having all these secret conversations and would stop talking every time I came into the room. I didn't think too much about it, as long as they weren't getting divorced, right? I figured Dad either found out something or was doing something not altogether legal on the side that involved the company, and someone found out about it. He was always kind of shiesty like that…"

She sniffed and drained the rest of the bottle. "The next thing I knew, Deputy Quintanar's at our house, and Mom's telling me to go hide. I start to climb into the crawl space above my bathroom, and then I hear a pistol shot, so I go down to see if Mom needs any help. I came in just in time to see her…see her get shot…"

She angrily wiped tears away. "I want that bastard to go to jail, or die for what he did to my parents."

"I can't guarantee either of those things are going to happen, but I'll do everything I can to bring them to justice."

The cruiser's red-and-blue lights came on behind them, but there was no siren yet. Bolan glanced at her. "If you've got yourself together, take the wheel. Keep driving straight south."

She gaped at him but moved over the center console to grab the wheel. "Where are you going?"

"To get rid of our tail." Bolan pointed to a button on the steering wheel. "When I tell you to, hit that."

He slid over the top of the driver's seat into the back, where he'd seen a Mossberg 590 shotgun on the seat. He checked the cruiser, which was coming ever closer, lights flashing, but not making any move to try to run them off the road—yet. Bolan lowered both passenger windows on the back doors, then checked the load in the shotgun. Three-inch rifled slugs. He racked the slide, then climbed into the third seat and braced himself. "Okay, press that button and brace yourself—this is going to be loud!"

The rear liftgate of the Caddy began to lower, letting in a blast of cold night air. As soon as Bolan saw the cruiser's hood, he unloaded on it, holding the Mossberg's trigger down and cycling the pump so that he emptied the entire 8-round magazine in just over three seconds.

The front end of the cruiser disintegrated. The grille splintered apart under the heavy slugs, which continued on to blow the radiator to pieces, spraying coolant like green blood over the pavement. The hood sprang up, blocking the entire windshield. Belts shredded as the fan blades flew apart, ricocheting off the crankcase and slicing through fluid lines. Both tires blew at almost the exact same time, shrapnel from the blown-apart engine shredding them to pieces. The car juked left, then right as it skidded to a stop in the middle of the road, smoking and steaming. The deputies scrambled out of the wreck, clawing their pistols out, but the Escalade was already out of range.

"Raise it!" The liftgate closed again, and Bolan walked down the narrow aisle past the two rows of seats to the front passenger chair. Still keeping the SUV on the road, Kelly shook her head. "What the hell was that?" she asked loudly.

Bolan's ears were ringing, too. Even with the windows down, the Mossberg packed quite a wallop. "A surefire way to get rid of a tailgater."

She stared at him, then smiled thinly. "Did you get either of them?"

"Nope, I wanted to make sure they weren't able to keep coming after us. Don't worry, I'm sure we haven't seen the last of them. If you really want your chance at Quintanar, you'll probably get it." He watched her digest that news, pleased to see she wasn't still spitting fire and expletives, but seeming to actually consider the idea, and what might happen.

Kelly checked the rearview mirror as she slowed to a respectable speed. "Okay, what next?"

"We have to get off the main roads. I hope you know the backcountry."

"Yeah, out here there's nothing to do but drive up and down these roads and get shit-faced in cornfields. You could say I know the area pretty damn well."

"Good. Get us back to the Miracle Mile Motel, on the north side of town. We'll hole up there while I get in touch with my people." Bolan reached for the satellite phone clipped to his belt, but when he tried to activate it, he realized he was holding a worthless piece of plastic. One of the close calls had been almost too close—a bullet had pierced the bottom part of the phone, shattering it. "Got a cell on you?"

Kelly slapped her pockets. "Crap, it's in my purse back at the house. Sorry."

Bolan frowned. "I thought you kids didn't go anywhere without those things nowadays."

She glared at him. "What can I say? I've been a bit distracted, what with men invading my house, killing my parents and shooting the place up…" She stared out the windshield for a moment. "God, that sounded crass, even for me."

Bolan reached out and patted her shoulder. "I know, but for the next little bit, that's what's going to keep you going. I don't know when you'll have time to cry for your mom and dad, but it probably won't be for a while, so save that grief until the time is right."

"What the hell am I supposed to do in the meantime?"

Bolan smiled, a thin-lipped grin with no warmth in it

whatsoever. "For the time being, I'd suggest turning it to anger at the men who did this to your family."

Kelly grinned back, more of a baring of her teeth than anything. "I can do that."

7

Deputy Rojas Quintanar watched the Escalade vanish into the darkness, still stunned by the complete reversal of fortune he'd suffered over the past ten minutes. What should have been a simple recovery had turned into a true debacle, with three men dead and his brother badly injured. And to top it all off, one man had done all this damage.

He heard a dull whoompf come from underneath the remains of the cruiser, and looked over to see fire licking up through the shattered engine compartment as some errant spark ignited leaking gasoline. He stared at the car, shook his head, then opened the driver's door, got his hat and placed it securely on his head.

His brother, shotgun still in hand, stared at him. "Shouldn't we put this out?"

"Call it in for the goddamn fire department, I've got fucking bigger problems to deal with." As he said that, bright halogen headlights lit up the night as a vehicle approached from the north. Quintanar glanced up to see the one SUV he least wanted to at that moment.

The black Escalade ESV glided to a stop behind the now blazing cruiser. The tinted passenger window slid down to reveal the face of Quintanar's boss, Feliz De Cavallos.

"Rojas, Maximo, good to see you're both all right. Our

guard saw the activity on the road and radioed it in. I thought I'd come out personally and see how you're taking care of our…interests."

Quintanar opened his mouth to speak, but De Cavallos raised his hand. "Why don't you get inside, and we'll discuss this on the way back to town?" Both rear passenger doors swung open.

Exchanging an apprehensive look with his brother, the deputy accepted the invitation, climbing in behind the passenger seat while his brother got in behind the driver. The doors swung shut without their having to touch them, and De Cavallos swiveled his captain's chair around to face the two men.

For his part, Quintanar was acutely aware of the walled-off cargo area at his back. No one had ever found out what was inside—at least, and lived to tell about it. Rumors ran the gamut from it housing some kind of mobile artillery or heavy machine gun platform to a personal torture chamber that De Cavallos used for interrogation or for simply inflicting pain. Personally, Quintanar hoped it was the former.

Taking a deep breath, he said, "I've already put out an APB on the company vehicle and have scrambled all off-duty officers to set up roadblocks on all roads accessing town. Our people are handling the scene for the Bitterman house, and the survivors are also getting medical attention."

"Yes, I noticed that of the men killed and injured three were ours. Your brother, while severely wounded, will apparently survive."

Quintanar breathed an internal sigh of relief at the news, but he also caught the undertone in De Cavallos's voice. "Sir, everyone at the site did everything they could to apprehend the girl and this Agent Cooper. Unfortunately, he was very skilled."

"Are you saying that he was better than all of you?"

"Well, he did manage to fight his way through six men,

rescue the girl that we had in our custody and escape." Quintanar didn't go any further.

"So what makes you think you'll be able to capture him if your paths cross a second time?"

A thin smile split the deputy's face. "Because he cannot take on the entire town." He grabbed the microphone on his lapel and spoke into it. "Dispatch, this is Rojas. Issue a BOLO alert for Matt Cooper and Kelly Bitterman, last seen heading south on Highway 22 in a black company Escalade, license plate Whiskey-Foxtrot-Tango-Five-Nine-Zero. Will be creating a bulletin for all local media with general description in next two hours. Have a sketch artist waiting when I return."

De Cavallos didn't say a word, but just sat back and watched Quintanar as he spoke. When the deputy was finished, his boss leaned forward. "What makes you think he isn't in the next county by now, heading for the nearest sheriff's department or police station?"

Quintanar didn't drop his gaze, but stared the other man right in the eye. "With what proof? A teenage girl who's already been in trouble as his only eyewitness? Plus, he's not the type to cut and run. He's going to stay around to find whatever he thinks he needs to take us all down. I don't know how to describe it, but it's almost like he's taking this personally...like it doesn't matter that he stumbled into something that should be making him call for backup, he's going to see it through to the end himself." Quintanar smiled again. "That kind of attitude is definitely going to get him killed."

Quintanar's boss didn't reply for a moment, leaving the deputy wondering about his silence. *He looks like I just confirmed something for him,* he thought. Just when Quintanar was about to continue, De Cavallos spoke. "For your sake, I hope so. Given what has just happened, you seem very confident that you'll be seeing him again."

"That son of a bitch embarrassed me and almost killed my brother. He's putting everything we've built here at risk. You're damn right I'm going to track him down, and bring you his head."

De Cavallos regarded the deputy for a moment, then nodded. "That is exactly what I expected to hear. Of course, I will be reinforcing the sheriff's department with Cristobal security. Our men will be sweeping through town, looking for any sign of this Matt Cooper. There will be no capturing him alive. Standing orders will be to shoot on sight."

Quintanar exchanged a dark, satisfied look with his brother. "That's just fine with us, sir. I only hope we find him first."

De Cavallos nodded. "If you do, then you will have the chance to avenge the stain on your honor. I don't care who does it, but Agent Cooper will not be leaving this town alive."

BOLAN GLANCED BACK, making sure no one was on their tail. "Can you get us back to that side road that runs past your place without using the highway?"

"Sure—why?"

"Gotta stash the backup wheels and pick up my gear."

Despite the drive, they weren't that far away from the Cadillac, and Kelly's expert knowledge of the back roads brought them to it in less than ten minutes. Bolan had kept his eyes open along the way, and once he was in the rental, drove it back to an obviously abandoned farmhouse with a leaning, once-red barn, its bright color faded underneath years of relentless of sun and wind. Shoving the door open, Bolan backed the SUV inside, then grabbed his bags, rear-ranged a few things and locked the vehicle. He walked out, closed the door, and glancing around to make sure no one had seen what he was up to, took a few minutes to wipe away the tire tracks in the dusty driveway.

When he got back in, he handed the Caddy's keys and electronic fob to Kelly. "If for some reason we get separated or things go bad, you come back here, take the SUV and drive for the next county police, you hear me? If you don't feel comfortable with that, head to your nearest relatives. There's two thousand dollars in the compartment between the front seats. That should be enough to get you just about anywhere you need to go. Now let's head back to town."

As Kelly took a roundabout way back into town, Bolan held the dead gunman's cell phone in his hand, weighing the risks of using it. He was pretty sure the crew at Stony Man Farm would be able to scramble the conversation, but there was always the possibility that the bad guys might be advanced enough to be able to triangulate his position while it was in use. No matter what, he'd be ditching it after the call, which would seriously hinder his ability to remain in contact with the Farm.

Keeping an eye on his watch, Bolan flipped the phone open and dialed the access number. Kurtzman's voice answered on the first ring. "Is this line secure?"

"No, we've got about two minutes."

"Initiating security communication protocols." Bolan heard a distant hum in the phone's speaker—their conversation was now scrambled, although the phone's activation would still show up on the grid. "Bought us another minute, maybe two. What the hell's going on out there, Striker? We lost your sat phone signal ten minutes ago—blackbox said it had suffered 'unknown damage,' and didn't know if you were alive or dead."

"Things have gotten a lot more complicated since we last spoke." Bolan quickly outlined the events of the past hour or so, ending with the destruction of the cruiser. "The witness to the parents' shooting is with me, and we're holing up for a bit until I can plan my next move. I don't know what's going on here, but whatever it is, it's deep, and the people behind it are very well financed and organized. By the way, I've got another hack job for Akira. I turned on the Bitterman's home computer, so have him get into it and see if Jack kept any personal records about what he was doing or what the company is up to. Other than that, I don't have any more intel—you got any light you can shed on this?"

"Not on Cristobal Pharmaceuticals. If they're dirty, they've got a great PR firm working for them. There hasn't been a whiff of any wrongdoing in the past five years. Of course, records south of the border are much spottier, but even our law-enforcement contacts in Central and South America haven't come up with anything solid yet. Give me another twenty-four hours and I might come up with something, but by that time you'll probably have destroyed the whole organization. As for your deputy, that's another story."

"Do tell. Wait a sec." Bolan glanced at Kelly as they swung off the road onto a narrow dirt trail. "What's going on?"

"Roadblock over the hill, so we're going around. Don't worry, I know the folks that own this land. We kids do it all the time."

Bolan looked at her with new respect. "How'd you know the road was blocked?"

"You can see through the two hills over here if you know where to look. It's a speed trap, and only catches the folks who don't know about it."

"Good eye." Bolan returned to his conversation. "Go."

"Quintanar, Rojas Esteban Arroyo, served in the Colombian military, fighting the counterinsurgency war against FARC in the midnineties. He quit in 1999, and headed north to the U.S.A. He's one of three brothers, and apparently liked what he saw once he got here, because he brought them all up, too."

"What? How in the hell did these guys get U.S. citizenship that quickly?"

"They either have masterfully forged documents, a lot of palms were greased, or maybe a little bit of both. We're still checking ICE records in Homeland Security to see if these guys are flagged, but so far they've kept their noses amazingly clean."

"Yeah, until tonight."

"Maybe so, but the county force is twelve men strong, and right now we should probably assume they're all out hunting for you. I think it's best that we pull you in, then regroup and hit these guys hard."

"Normally I'd agree with you, but they're already on alert. If we give them even twelve hours, they'll clean up anything incriminating and meet us with open arms, empty computers and no evidence, and shrug when we accuse them of anything. Besides, I still don't know what the hell's going on here. It's a lot more than just some corrupt deputies, but I want some kind of proof so I can take down these scum once and for all. If I just walk away—" Bolan's gaze flicked to Kelly "—at least two people will have died for nothing."

"That sounds like a tall order, Striker. I know you've come through hellfire before, but you're on unfamiliar terrain and surrounded by the enemy."

"Maybe, but their control of the town has made them overconfident. Besides, they have to cover the whole area looking for me, while I'm staying mobile, moving light and fast. By morning I should have everything I'll need to really bring in the DOJ to clean this up."

"The boss is going to raise his eyebrows at this lone wolf bit."

"They started it, so I'm just going to finish it. And Hal knows that I do what I have to do. Gotta go, our time's up."

"Striker, you know I have to call in reinforcements, especially since this is an unsanctioned op. You gonna remain on this cell?"

"Can't. Too many unfriendly ears around. I'll call in again in a few hours." Bolan hung up, then slid off the battery cover. Unplugging the battery, he lowered the window and threw it out, then slid out the SIM chip, broke it in two, and did the same a half mile down the road. The rest of the phone followed a minute later.

Kelly cast furtive glances around as they came to an intersection on the north side of town. "We're coming back in. You might want to keep your head down."

Bolan didn't slouch one inch. "That's why I chose the Miracle Mile on this side of town. It's the one on your left. My room is number 9."

"Says the guy who's only been here a day to the girl who's grown up here her whole life." Kelly rolled her eyes as she pulled into the parking lot, driving around back and nosing the Escalade into a space in the empty lot. "I'm dying for a shower."

"It's all yours. Just let me make sure the room's secure first." Bolan leaned down and checked to make sure the hair he'd pasted to the door with saliva was still attached to the jamb. Sometimes the simplest alarm systems were still the best, he noted, casually glancing around. Other than a skinny Hispanic kid pushing a cleaning cart down at the other end of the motel, the place was deserted. "Okay, let's go."

Bolan inserted his key in the lock and opened the door, pushing it as he walked into the room. A shadow moved in the moonlight to his right, and he smelled a familiar cologne.

Shit.

As he reached for the Beretta, he felt a small circle of cold steel press into his temple, and a familiar voice mocked him.

"Please give me a reason to pull this trigger, amigo."

8

Bolan tensed for a moment, wanting to disarm the arrogant punk and pushing his face into the nearest wall. It wouldn't be difficult. Putting a gun this close to a target's head was practically an invitation to have it taken away, and Bolan knew a half-dozen ways to do so in under two seconds.

"Who's— Hey, what are you doing? Let me go!" Kelly's panicking voice behind him made Bolan's decision for him. He relaxed and slowly moved his hand away from the pistol.

The Beretta was snatched from its holster. "Set the bag down, slowly, and walk to the center of the room."

The lights came on as he did so, and once he had reached the middle of the room Bolan turned, blinking in the glare. Everado De Cavallos stood by the door, pointing a big, chrome pistol at Bolan's face. Two more of his crew Bolan recognized from that afternoon shoved Kelly through the door, closing it behind them. The soldier sensed another person come out of the bathroom, and realized the whole gang was here. Kelly sank into a cloth-and-wooden chair near the door, the two who had escorted her taking up positions on either side of her.

"Well, well, look what we have here—the man the entire sheriff's department couldn't catch. And who's this with him? The little bitch that gave Deputy Quintanar the slip yesterday." Everado chuckled, his laughter picked up by the rest of his followers. Suddenly the young man's expression turned serious. "I can't wait to see what they say when we bring these two in gift wrapped."

Bolan took them by surprise by speaking. "You're pretty good, I'll give you that. How'd you find us?"

The four youths burst out laughing, although Everado's gun never wavered from Bolan's head. Finally, Everado waved at the others to shut up. "Man, have you ever been in a small town? Everyone knows everything here. My homie working the cleaning crew gave me the 411 on you checking in this afternoon after I spread your picture around to my boys. He let me and Carlos in through the back window, and Luis and Paco took the rooms on either side, to make sure you didn't book out the front. Once we were all in position, all we had to do was stay awake until you came back. Too easy."

Guess those old security methods don't work as well as I'd thought, Bolan concluded. "Better than I expected from four small-town punks, that's for sure."

Everado's face darkened, and he stepped closer to Bolan, thumbing back the hammer on his SIG-Sauer. "I'd watch that shit if I were you. No one said you had to go to Cristobal in one piece, gringo."

"Look, you guys don't want to do this. My name is Matt Cooper, and I'm a federal agent with the Department of Justice, Domestic Security Section. That deputy who bailed you out earlier today is already in a lot of trouble, and I don't think you boys want to go down with him." Bolan slowly lowered his right hand and held it out. "Why don't you give me the gun, and we can talk this over?"

The four boys exchanged glances again, then they all burst out laughing even harder than before. While they were yukking it up, Bolan exchanged his own glance with Kelly.

Although her lips were tight with fear, she also had a free hand dangling near the black canvas bag Bolan had dropped near the door. Her eyes flicked down at it, then up at him again. Bolan shook his head, then lifted his gaze to the cheap light fixture overhead. Staring at her, he waited to see if she understood his message. She frowned, then nodded just as Everado feigned wiping a tear from his eye and shook his head.

"You sure you're not a fucking comedian? You have no fucking idea what you're in the middle of, do you?"

"Why don't you enlighten me?"

As Bolan figured, the kid couldn't resist the bait. "Dumbass *norteamericano,* you accidentally stumbled into the biggest drug lab in the state, probably in the country, all operating under your *estupido* government's very nose. We're running tons of the shit out of here every week, and nobody knows jack about it. Oh, your DEA agents know that hundreds of pounds of high-grade stuff are swarming out of the middle of your country, but they have no idea where to look. They still think it's Charley Blue-Collar cooking it up in his basement or an RV. It's the fucking perfect setup. Shit, we just should have thought of it years ago."

Bolan nodded. "So Cristobal makes the dying town of Quincyville an offer it can't refuse, right? It sets up its headquarters nearby, bringing jobs and economic prosperity to the area. And in return all it wants to do is run what, coke, meth out of the location to your distributors around the country? Pretty slick."

Everado nodded as Bolan summarized the operation. "Hey, you got it, homes. And you know what the best thing about it is? Since Cristobal's a pharmaceutical company, we make the pseudoephedrine that we use in the meth production! No worries about trying to acquire mass quantities!"

The four boys laughed again. When the laughter died down once again, Everado took a firmer grip on his pistol.

"So you see, we aren't worried about a lone federal agent out here. There's a million miles of fuckin' prairie to bury you under, although since they have all that acid and shit at the company, I doubt anyone's ever gonna find your body once my father's done with you."

"Your father's head of security at Cristobal?"

Everado frowned in puzzlement. "Yeah, why?"

"Because I spoke to him earlier this evening."

"Oh, you two have a good chat?"

Bolan's expression turned ice-cold. "I doubt he thought so. I talked to him right after I'd killed three of his men and told him I was coming for him next."

Everado grinned again, glancing at his boys. "You got *co-jones,* that's for sure, *federale.* I might want to stick around, see how long it takes him to break you."

"You won't want to see that, trust me."

The younger De Cavallos sobered. "Maybe I do, maybe I don't." He shook his head again. Given that and Everado's twitchiness, Bolan had already pegged him for at least a casual meth user, maybe about to take it to the next level.

"That's enough fun and games. Time to take you and the bitch here in for interrogation."

Bolan glanced over at Kelly. "Now."

She reached up behind the thug on her right and hit the light switch, plunging the room into darkness. Bolan ducked as Everado's pistol flashed and roared, the bullet passing over his head.

Crouching, the soldier lashed out with his heel at where Everado's shins should have been. He was rewarded with a meaty impact and a grunt of pain, followed by a heavy thump as the punk hit the floor. Bolan was already heading toward the door, where two figures silhouetted against the parking lot light fought with a snarling, kicking wildcat in the chair. One of them reached over and flipped on the room light just in time to see Bolan next to him, both hands raised in a hammer blow that came crashing down on the spot between his neck and shoulder. Stunned, the youth sank to the floor.

"Fuckin' shoot him!" Everado shouted as Bolan flicked the lights off again.

Kelly was doing everything in her power to fend off the second guard, but he was slowly overpowering her. Bolan drove a hard fist into the young man's kidney, making him groan and release her. Grabbing him by the shoulders, the soldier whipped him around, shoving him into the center of the room. He slammed into somebody—Everado, Bolan hoped—and they both fell to the floor in a huge crash.

"Out the door, let's go!" Bolan grabbed Kelly's arm with his right hand and the black bag with his left, slinging it over his shoulder so he could reach for the door. The bathroom light flicked on just as he got the door open.

"Freeze, both of you!" the fourth youth by the bathroom said. Bolan let go of Kelly just long enough to flick the room lights back on, then shoved her out the door, lunging out and to the left himself. Gunshots sounded behind him, but he was already hauling Kelly down the outside hallway and around the corner.

"Let go! I can run better without you draggin' me!" Kelly panted beside him, but once Bolan released her, she pulled ahead of him.

"Are you hurt? Were you shot anywhere?" Bolan asked as they ran.

"Don't think so…what's the plan?"

"Get to the Escalade and get the hell out of here. Those shots'll bring the deputies any minute."

"Don't you think they're gonna figure out where we're going?"

"Possibly, that's why we're moving fast. Come on." At the rear corner of the building, Bolan peeked around and saw no one near the SUV. "Stay low." He took a flash-bang grenade out of his bag and kept it ready as they crept underneath the first-floor windows of the other rooms toward their vehicle. As they approached, Bolan could hear Everado berating his boys for their incompetence.

They were only a few yards from the SUV when the bathroom window slid open. As a head started to poke out, Bolan stepped forward and grabbed the youth by his neck, pulling him out and slamming him to the ground. A shout from inside sounded a warning, but Bolan had already yanked the pin on his grenade and tossed it into the small room. He turned to Kelly. "Get in, and don't look behind you."

"What the— Holy sh—!" came from the room before bright white flashes could be seen, even facing away from the motel. They were followed immediately by a series of loud booms that rattled Bolan's ears. Anyone inside the room would have been almost completely deafened from the concussions.

"Time to go." Bolan slid behind the wheel and fired up the SUV. Backing out of the parking space, he pulled around to the front as three coughing figures stumbled out of the smoking room. Amazingly, one of them could still see well enough to spot the Escalade as they left the parking lot.

"You've got to be kidding," Bolan said as he watched the three run behind the manager's office, a freestanding building in front of where the guests stayed. Moments later, a silver Escalade tore out of the parking lot and onto the highway, heading after them.

Kelly glanced back at their pursuers. "Jeez, you sure get a lotta people pissed off at you."

Despite their situation, Bolan grinned. "Story of my life." He checked the rearview mirror, then noticed her climbing into the backseat. "What are you doing?"

"Making sure they don't catch us, that's what." She'd found the shotgun and a box of shells on the floor, and was deftly reloading it.

"Maybe I should do that."

Having finished feeding shells into the magazine, Kelly racked the slide with practiced ease. "No, you keep driving. If they ram us, I think you'd be able to handle it better. You'll be coming up on Sandy Lane. Turn left onto it."

Sure enough, the silver Escalade roared right up to their bumper, then crashed into it, jarring the entire vehicle. Everado, his eyes red and teary, stuck his head and gun out the passenger window and let loose with a flurry of rounds, none of them even coming close to the SUV.

Bolan shook his head. "Those flash-bangs really screw with your vision. He won't be seeing straight for a while. Here's the turn—hang on!"

Bolan tapped the brake just enough to let the wheels grab the pavement as he guided the top-heavy SUV onto the single-lane road leading out into the prairie. Their pursuers almost overshot the intersection, and had to back up before they could tear off again after their quarry.

"Should we wait for them to catch up?" Bolan asked as he eyed them in the rear view mirror.

Kelly smirked. "They are kind of pathetic, aren't they?"

"Well, they weren't in the motel room. Good move with the lights, by the way. A lot of people wouldn't have had the guts to follow through with it."

Kelly snorted. "I sure wasn't going anywhere else with those assholes. I was more worried about you being stuck in the middle with Everado about to blow your brains out."

"I'm touched." The bright lights of the pursuing SUV finally filled the cab. "Here they come."

"I'm on it." Kelly held the slide and pistol grip of the shotgun with white-knuckled fingers, but she looked more than ready to let loose some hellfire. Bolan slowed the SUV a bit, letting the other one pull alongside, the two vehicles taking up the entire road.

"Almost there…"

Everado fired a shot that glanced off their hood. "Pull over, motherfuckers!" he shouted into the wind.

Kelly hit the electronic window control for the back window. As soon as she had enough room, she pointed the muzzle of the shotgun at the silver SUV's right front tire.

"Holy— Stop!" Everado barked at his driver, trying to swing around and aim his pistol at the same time. He was too late.

Kelly unloaded on the tire, shredding it, then pumped the slide and hit the right front fender, the slug punching through it into the engine.

The driver of the silver Escalade panicked and yanked his steering wheel hard right to get away from the onslaught. At that speed, there was only one way the SUV could go.

The luxury SUV rolled onto its side, then flipped over completely before coming to a stop lying on the passenger side, a total wreck, one wheel still spinning, and smoke drifting from its holed engine compartment.

"Sure hope Everado got back inside before that happened." Bolan executed a neat y-turn and drove back up to the broken SUV, illuminating it in his vehicle's headlights. A large bloodstain was plainly visible on the shattered windshield, and the left-turn signal flashed uselessly.

"Let me have that."

Kelly handed over the shotgun.

Bolan checked the load, then got out and slowly approached the other vehicle, his weapon at the ready. There were no signs of life, no moans or shouts for help. Reversing the gun, Bolan slammed the butt into the windshield, breaking it loose from the frame. Eventually, he had enough free that he could lever it out onto the road.

The driver was clearly dead, his face turned into a mask of blood and glass on his lolling head. A cell phone was still clipped into a hands-free holder plugged into the dashboard. Bolan grabbed it, then scanned for his real quarry. He almost didn't see Everado until he spotted a cowboy boot lying on the broken door window. The would-be south-of-the-border gangster had somehow gotten his entire body wedged into the passenger-side leg compartment. Reaching in, Bolan grabbed him by the arm and pulled none too gently until he had pried the kid's body out. As he did, something clattered to the ground.

"Figured that would show up again." Bolan picked up his Beretta 93-R, which had fallen from the kid's waistband, and tucked it into the holster at the small of his back.

He saw the splayed limbs of another body in the backseat of the SUV but didn't really care. He had the person he'd come for. Dragging Everado's limp body back to his Escalade, Bolan opened the passenger door and checked the glove compartment. As he'd expected, he found heavy plastic zip ties. Trussing the young man's arms and legs, he carried him to the cargo area and tossed him inside, then got back behind the wheel and drove away.

9

Quintanar was on his third cup of coffee in the past hour as he coordinated every aspect of the search from one end of town to the other. They had put out the bulletin to the local radio and television station, and teams of two men were scouring the town and every house in a five-mile radius.

The only promising lead had been an apparent disturbance at the Miracle Mile Motel that involved shots fired at the location. By the time Quintanar and heavy reinforcements had gotten there, the place was a mess of activity, with the few remaining guests milling around among the fire department vehicles and an ambulance, which had been called out to investigate a call of smoke coming from one of the rooms.

After confirming that the room was secure and the building was in no danger of igniting, Quintanar had walked through the room with the firemen. He found a bullet hole in the back wall about four feet off the floor, and evidence of another that had gouged out a chunk of the door frame as it had passed. He noticed no blood anywhere, just overturned furniture and evidence of a scuffle. Well, that and the bullet holes and some kind of incendiary device, he thought. Somebody decided to raise the stakes, and I bet I know exactly who that was. The deputy took pictures of the damage, then shot the rest of the room with his digital camera before heading to the bathroom.

A twisted, charred piece of metal under the sink caught his eye. Quintanar squatted to take a closer look. He'd already suspected what had happened from the smell, and the metal confirmed his theory. Someone had set off a flash-bang grenade in here. He shook his head. It had to have been an eardrum-shattering thunderclap in this enclosed space. He pulled out a plastic bag from his pocket and used a pen to sweep the fragment into the bag. He examined the rest of the floor, finding several more fragments, and bagged them as well.

A voice called through the window. "Hey, Deputy, we got a victim outside, below the window."

Quintanar rose and carefully peered out the window at a young man sitting on the concrete parking marker, rubbing the back of his head. "Keep him there."

He strode outside and around the building to the young man, whom he recognized as one of Everado's crew. Quintanar pulled the paramedic, a plumpish but efficient woman named MacReady, aside. "How's he look?"

"Banged up, but otherwise all right. His face got scraped by the pavement—apparently when he used it to break his fall out the window—and he's got a good-sized lump on the back of his head. If I were the overly cautious type, I'd probably run an X-ray to see if he got a concussion, but he's not displaying any of the typical symptoms. I think he took a knock to the skull that rattled him, but he should be all right with a good night's rest. He'll probably have a hell of a headache for the next couple days."

"All right, thanks. If he's okay to be released to me, I think you're pretty much done here."

She nodded. "Thanks, Rojas."

He walked over to the kid and stared down at him. "*Hola*, Luis."

The kid started at hearing his name, glancing up with a sheepish expression. "*Hola,* sir."

"Mind telling me what went down here this night?"

Luis filled him in on Everado's plan to catch the gringo. For his part, Quintanar wasn't surprised. It had all the hallmarks of the younger De Cavallos—long on guts, short on brains. Beyond that, Luis couldn't tell him anything else, not even which way they had gone. After making sure the kid was okay to drive, the deputy sent him home, telling him he'd follow up with any more questions in the morning.

Interrogating the motel owner also proved worthless. All he knew was that a man matching the description on the radio had checked in earlier that afternoon, but he hadn't seen him recently. The boy cleaning the rooms, however, was a fount of information. He confirmed that Everado De Cavallos had paid him one hundred dollars to let the young thug and his group set up in the agent's room to capture him when he returned. The ambush had gone wrong, and the American had escaped, along with a teenage girl. They had taken off north in an Escalade, followed by Everado and his remaining boys.

Admirably restraining his anger at having them slip through his fingers a second time, Quintanar was just pulling onto the highway when dispatch radioed him about a 911 call received from Sandy Lane, a mile west of the highway. It involved a silver Escalade, matching the description of the one Everado had been in, that had overturned on the road.

Quintanar had hit his lights and sped out there, but arrived too late once again. Of the rest of the flunkies, only one had survived, and he was seriously injured. There was no sign of their leader. Quintanar had tried Everado's cell phone number, but it had gone straight to voice mail. That was slightly heartening—it probably meant the little *pendejo* was still alive somewhere.

Quintanar made sure the area was cordoned off and the

paramedics got the lone survivor off to the Quincyville hospital. Next he called the nearest three teams and executed a search of the nearby plains, just in case Everado had been injured and wandered off into a field. When they'd turned up no sign of him, he'd had them fan out and search every house in a three-mile radius, looking for that black Escalade. Once again he silently cursed De Cavallos's rejection of his plan to outfit every company vehicle with GPS trackers. Should have gone ahead and done it anyway, then we'd be on our way to finding him instead of running around with our heads up our asses, he thought.

Shaking his head, he pulled out his cell phone and speed-dialed the senior De Cavallos's number. *"Si?"*

"It's Quintanar, sir." The deputy brought him up to speed on the situation, including the search efforts for his son.

Despite his personal stake in the matter, De Cavallos was all business. "Based on what you've found, what do you think happened to my son?"

Quintanar didn't hesitate. The man may have been a dick to work for, but he respected family ties. Rojas wasn't about to yank his chain on this. "It's very likely that the American has taken him hostage, sir. Have you tried contacting him recently?"

"Yes. The call always goes to voice mail. I know you'll do everything in your power to recover my son alive. Keep me informed, and remember that all Cristobel facilities are at your disposal."

"Thank you sir, we'll find your son, I promise."

Quintanar disconnected the call, then contacted his search teams via walkie-talkie. No one had found anything yet. He told them all to keep looking and contact him the moment anyone found any lead, no matter how slight. Climbing back into his Dodge Ramcharger, he racked his brain, trying to work out how a total stranger could disappear so quickly into the countryside. He quickly reviewed where he had seen Cooper—outside the diner, and at the…

"Newspaper!" He took off back into town, pulling into the *Gazette*'s parking lot a few minutes later. A lone light burned in the building. Quintanar got out of his car and rapped on the glass of the main door. A frizzy-haired man rose from his desk and peered out at the deputy.

"Yeah."

"I'm looking for the editor, Casey Hinder."

"She's gone home for the evening."

"Okay, thanks." Tamping down his increasing irritation, Quintanar called dispatch and got the address of the Hinder home. Driving there took less than five minutes. The Hinders lived in a neat trailer with a postage-stamp sized lawn on the north side of town. Lights were on in the kitchen and at one end of the trailer.

Quintanar got out of his car, put his hat on and climbed the wooden steps to the front door on the side of the home. He knocked, then stepped back and waited. The light next to the door came on, and the inner door opened to reveal Casey Hinder behind the screen.

"Deputy Quintanar, what can I do for you? I don't think my daughter has any more information for you than what she told you this afternoon."

"Good evening, Ms. Hinder. I'm sorry to bother you this late at night, however, you're who I came to see."

"Really? Why?"

"It has to do with that man you met earlier today, Matt Cooper."

She frowned. "Yes, he stopped by the newspaper office. What does this have to do with me?"

"Have you been watching television or listening to the radio recently?" Quintanar asked.

"To be honest, I deal with the media all day long, so the

last thing I really want to do is see more of it when I come home. Why?"

"It turns out that Mr. Cooper is a felon who has already committed several crimes in our town, including assault against several deputies, and kidnapping, I'm afraid."

The woman's hands flew to her mouth. "Oh my God? What can I do to help?"

"I'd like you to come down to the station and get an official statement about the conversation that you had with him. Would you mind?"

"No, no, of course not. Just let me tell my daughter where I'll be. Just a moment." The door closed, and Quintanar heard muffled conversation for a few moments, then she reappeared in a jean jacket, with a purse under her arm. "Let's go."

10

Everado De Cavallos awoke to pitch-blackness. In his dis-
oriented state, for the first few moments he couldn't tell if
he was conscious or still dreaming. Blinking his eyes, he
felt one lid move slowly, sticky with what he hoped was only
sweat and not blood.

His entire body felt like it had been thrown into a brick
wall—everything hurt from his head to his toes. His right
arm throbbed particularly hard, but when he tried to move it
to check how badly it was damaged, it resisted his attempt.
Pulling harder only sent sharp pains through his wrists,
which were pinioned to his sides.

Breathing hard, Everado pulled again, trying to move his
legs at the same time, but finding them secured too. He realized he was tied to a straight-backed kitchen chair. Straining his eyes to the limit only revealed more impenetrable
blackness.

Suddenly he heard a soft, high-pitched whine, as if some
kind of electronic device had just powered up. "Hey? Is
anyone there? Can you help me?"

A firm hand fell on his shoulder, making Everado jump
and cry out. "I could help you, Everado, but I don't think
you'd like it."

"Cooper? Is that you? Hey, man, if you're really Justice,

you can't do this to me. I know my rights. You gotta Miran-dize me, and give me a lawyer and at least a fucking phone call."

"Hmm, you're right. Where are my manners?" A bright light flashed in Everado's eyes, making him turn away from the glare. He felt something fall into his lap, and blinking, glanced down to see his own cell phone turned on with a speed-dial number appearing on the screen: Dad.

"I'll bet you want to push that call button really bad right now, don't you?" Bolan said. Despite himself, Everado realized he was straining down at the phone, trying desperately to reach it with his fingers, his nose, any way he could. He pulled as hard as he could, but the cell phone remained mad-deningly out of reach. After maybe a minute, the phone was snatched away and turned off. "Let the record show that the suspect refused his phone call."

"Hey, what the fuck—" was all Everado got out before a leather-gloved hand clamped tightly over his mouth. Everado felt warm breath on his neck and heard Cooper's cold voice whisper in his ear. "Shh—you asked for your rights, so I'm going to tell you what they are."

Everado tried even harder to break free, but his fingers were losing all feeling, and arching his back got him noth-ing but his head yanked back. Although his wrists were slick with sweat, he couldn't get either hand loose.

"I'd be careful if I were you, Everado. Try anything else, and you could be charged with resisting arrest. You're al-ready neck-deep in crap at the moment, and adding more charges could make things go even worse for you."

Breathing hard through his nose, Everado calmed, re-laxing into his chair again. "Good, good. Now, where were we? Ah, yes, your Miranda rights. You have the right to remain silent, however, be advised that I will use any and all methods of coercion to get you to waive that right and tell me everything I want to know. There's no way in hell I'm providing you a lawyer, but if you manage to survive this interrogation session, one can be appointed for you when you go to court. Do you understand these rights as I've explained them to you?"

The hand was removed, and Everado spluttered and spat before replying. "What the hell are you doing? You're a federal agent operating in the United States of America. You can't fucking treat me this way!" Sweat bloomed everywhere on his body, and his bladder tightened involuntarily.

"Yeah, about that…" The cell phone flared again, the light from the screen illuminating Bolan's head, which was half-covered by a high-tech set of night-vision goggles. "I'm afraid I may have misled you a bit. You see, I'm not a federal agent. I'm what you would call a freelancer, able to do whatever I please, whenever I please, wherever I please—and to whomever I please. You can consider this place my own private extraordinary rendition site. Now, since I'm a humane interrogator, I'll give you your choice of methods."

Everado heard a scrape, and then a red-orange flame burst into life a foot from his face, close enough for him to feel the heat radiating from it. The fire was coming from a self-contained portable blowtorch, held by Bolan, who was barely visible behind it. As Everado watched with wide eyes, Bolan adjusted the flame until it turned from a large red flame to a hissing blue jet of fire only a few inches long. "Your first choice is interrogation by fire…" Bolan twisted the knob, cutting the flame off and plunging the room back into darkness.

His nose wrinkling from the odor of the burned fuel, Everado heard him walking across the room, followed by the sound of something fairly heavy being set down on the floor with a thump. A second later, bright sparks flashed in front of his face, giving off just enough light to reveal Bolan's face, looking insectile and inhuman in the light from the two jumper cable wires he was touching together, the other ends attached to a car battery. "Or you can go with a little electroshock therapy."

Everado's bladder let go with a gush, spraying warm urine down his leg as he stared at the obvious psycho in front of him, his mouth opening and closing, but no sound coming out.

"Of course, you can prevent any further harm from coming to you if you tell me everything I want to know about your father, the Cristobal compound and your drug pipeline. I want names, locations, deliveries, associated companies, everything you can possibly think of."

Everado felt wetness stream down his cheeks and tasted salty tears. "You're fucking crazy, man! You can't do this to me! I'm a goddamn citizen of the sovereign nation of Mexico! I have rights, goddamn it!"

Bolan's nose wrinkled. "Pretty big talk coming from a guy who just wet his pants. I know exactly what you are, Everado. You're a parasite on the underbelly of this great nation, content to keep taking and taking and taking from it without giving anything back. You think you're entitled to this sweet life of yours? You just got lucky, winning the birth lottery and ending up the son of a drug dealer. I know of thousands of people on both sides of the border down south that are a hundred times more deserving of half the privileges you take for granted every single day. Nobody in America owes you a thing, and neither does your homeland. You gave up all your rights when you decided to profit from other people's misery and weakness."

Everado strained helplessly at his bonds. "Look—look, Cooper, listen to me, man. You're just one guy. You can't possibly beat everyone my father's bringing against you. Tell you what. You let me go right now, and maybe he'll let you live."

"Oh don't worry. I have unfinished business with your father, so I'll be paying him a visit very soon. Well, we should get started." He frowned before dragging the battery away from the pool underneath Everado's chair. "Don't want to risk electrocuting myself. Guess that means we're going with fire."

"Cooper, you're not serious… Hey man, you can't fucking do this!"

Bolan set the cables down off in the darkness and walked back toward Everado with slow, measured steps. The young punk was almost hyperventilating, and he couldn't help letting out a whimper when the black-haired man struck flint to the end of the blowtorch and made that bright golden-blue flame spurt out again.

Bolan walked around him slowly. "You ever smell burning skin? I'll bet you have, amigo. Maybe south of the border, visiting your grandparents in the summer, when they slaughtered chickens for dinner. They'd use a blowtorch—probably one just like this—to cauterize the neck stump after they chopped off the bird's head and it stopped flopping around. You never forget that smell—kind of sickly sweet, with a sort of metallic odor underneath. I bet that's the burning copper in the blood…" As he spoke, he adjusted the flame and brought it closer and closer to Everado's face, the bright blue fire growing larger and larger until it filled the young man's vision. He turned his head as far away as he could get, but it wasn't far enough. The flame kept coming closer… closer…closer…until Everado imagined he felt his eyebrows crisping under the intense heat.

"Okay, okay, okay, okay! Jesus, I'll tell you anything you want to know, just get that fucking thing away from me!"

The blue flame disappeared, and the room lights came on, making Everado blink tears away as he looked around. He was in a bare room with white walls, black garbage bags duct-taped over the two windows. The torch lay on the floor, next to the battery and jumper cables. His mask off, Bolan grabbed a kitchen chair identical to the one Everado was secured to. He set it down with the chair's back to Everado and straddled it, then held up a small digital recorder to the young man's mouth.

"Start talking."

BOLAN WALKED OUT of the room thirty minutes later, tapping the recorder in his hand thoughtfully. Kelly sat on a battered couch in the living room of the safehouse Bolan had rented, leafing through an old copy of *Guns & Ammo*. She'd found an old portable radio and had turned it on, the electronic, overdubbed Top 40 music blaring.

His eyebrows rose. "I thought you'd be asleep."

She glanced up at him. "Kind of hard to sleep around here, what with all of the shouting and carrying on in the next room. Walls are paper-thin here."

"Sorry. You might want to check the bedroom down the hall. Our associate isn't going anywhere for the time being."

Kelly frowned. "Sounded pretty rough in there at the beginning. You didn't, uh, you know…"

"Torture him?" Bolan shook his head. "Not physically. Psychologically, well…I needed to break him fast, and this was the best way to do it. That bother you?"

She shrugged. "I…don't know. If he was still resisting, would you have done the, you know, the physical stuff?"

Bolan paused for a moment before answering. "That's for me to know, and you to hopefully never have to find out." He would never actually go physical on people he was trying to get information from—that kind of stuff was for television dramas, not to mention the fact that intel gained that way was often seriously compromised—but he also couldn't risk her accidentally spilling that information to Everado or someone else. "By the way, thanks for the assist earlier tonight. Where'd you learn to handle a shotgun like that?"

Kelly shook her head like Bolan was always one step behind. "You're in Kansas now, Dorothy. Growing up out here involves learning to crawl, walk, shoot, then run—in that order."

"Well, God bless America." The glimmer of an idea was sparking in Bolan's mind—something about what she had just said, but it hadn't fully formed yet. He'd let it percolate for a bit yet, no doubt if it was workable, he'd know it soon enough. He regarded the girl for a moment, but she was suddenly engrossed in the radio, picking it up and listening intently.

"What time is it?"

Bolan checked his watch. "Just after ten p.m."

"Listen to this." She turned up the volume as Bolan walked toward the couch.

And here's your news at the top of the hour. Sheriff's deputies are still looking for the fugitive known as Matt Cooper, wanted in relation to the alleged murders of Jack and Sandra Bitterman two days ago. The deputies are also seeking him in connection to the disappearance of the Bittermans' daughter, Kelly, who hasn't been seen since the night of the shooting. Residents are advised to be on the lookout for a man in his mid-to late thirties, with short black hair and blue eyes. He stands approximately six feet, three inches tall, and weighs approximately two hundred pounds. Photos of him can be seen at the sheriff's department website, www.ECSD.com. He was last seen driving a black Cadillac Escalade, license number WFT-590. Authorities have warned to use extreme caution, and not to approach this man if he is spotted, as he is armed and extremely dangerous. Anyone seeing him should immediately contact the sheriff's department at 555-8429. Now for your KQIN weather report…

"Well, De Cavallos certainly has upped the ante, hasn't he?" Taking out Everado's cell phone, Bolan flipped through its menus, then pressed a button. "Keep quiet."

Putting the phone to his ear, he waited until the person on the other end picked up. "Everado? *¿Dónde estás?*"

"This isn't your son, Mr. De Cavallos. This is Matt Cooper."

He listened to the silence on the other end before the man found his voice. "Where is Everado?"

"He's safe—"

"I want to hear from him. Put him on the line."

"Sure." Bolan pressed the Play button on the digital recorder. Everado's voice came out. "Father, I'm being held against my will—"

Bolan took the recorder away and pressed Pause. "That's all you get right now. However, I assure you that he's perfectly fine. He decided to come looking for me after our little conversation outside the diner. Unfortunately, his friend wasn't a very good driver, and he was involved in a nasty auto accident. I thought it would be best to take him into custody for his own protection."

"What do you want, Mr. Cooper?"

Bolan had to give the man credit—he hadn't blustered or threatened, but just got right to the point. He decided to return the favor. "I want you to pack up your Cristobal company and head out of town. South of the border will be fine. You have six hours to comply. If you do, and prove it to my satisfaction, I will release your son unharmed. If you don't, I will be forced to take more punitive measures."

"I cannot close down the company in your time frame. The manufacturing lines alone cannot be stopped until the current run is complete—"

"That's not my problem. You have six hours to shut it down completely, or I'll shut it down for you. I'll be in touch soon to check on your progress."

Bolan snapped the phone closed and powered it down. Kelly stared at him. "Are you crazy?"

"No." Bolan walked to the end of the house. "I don't know about you, but I'm going to get a few hours' sleep. You probably should, too."

"Why?"

"Because when I get up, I'm going on the offensive."

11

Heriberto Pinilla and Amador Salegio had been cruising the back roads around Quincyville for the past three hours, and both hired guns were tired and bored.

Each had come from a small village in the heart of Mexico, and each had joined the military as soon as he could, escaping the soul-crushing poverty that was sucking the life out of their families. Both men had learned how to fight in the army, and also how to speak English fairly fluently. And they had one other thing in common—once they'd gotten a taste of the easy money that could be made looking the other way while drugs were smuggled across the border, they were both hooked. And when their military service was at an end, they had immediately used their cartel connections to hire themselves out to whomever needed them.

That was how they'd ended up in Quincyville as part of the security detail for Cristobal Pharmaceuticals. The perks of the job were pure heaven—living in an American town with all of its luxuries at their fingertips, including air-conditioning, electricity 24/7 and clean, fresh water whenever they wanted it. They got to tool around in fine vehicles like this Escalade, only a year old and with power and comfort to spare, and got their choice of weapons when they needed them.

There was only one problem with the position—there was very little to *do* in terms of security. Heriberto and Amador had been in Quincyville more than a year, and they'd had only two real jobs of any import—one had been chasing down a truck driver who'd been stupid enough to try to steal an entire shipment, and the other had been following one of the salesmen when he'd been suspected of informing on the company. They'd caught him, and ended up killing him and disposing of his body in an acid bath.

That had all changed earlier this evening. Their boss, De Cavallos—a man for whom both would willingly lay down their lives—had called them and every other security man, on or off duty, into a conference room and laid out the current mission for them. An American federal agent was snooping around in town, and he had to be located and taken out immediately. Earlier that evening he'd killed three Cristobal security men, wounded one town deputy, kidnapped the only witness to the Bitterman incident and stolen a company Escalade. Standing orders were to capture him alive if possible, but dead would work just as well. De Cavallos had ordered everyone to pull bulletproof vests from the armory, divided them into teams and assigned them areas of town to search, subject to reassignment by the sheriff's department as needed.

However, the thrill of hunting a wanted fugitive had soon since been replaced by the tedium of driving up and down deserted back roads, checking isolated houses one by one for the stolen SUV. The first hour they had been on the alert, tracking every small sound and rare flash of distant headlights. But as the night had worn on, they had grown a bit more complacent, to the point where Heriberto had stopped the SUV to urinate when he had spotted the narrow driveway that led over a small hill. Zipping up, he'd grabbed a flashlight and checked the worn ruts, finding recent tread marks in the dust that matched the tires on their own SUV.

He'd told Amador, and they'd turned off the Escalade's headlights and used their night-vision goggles to guide them as they slowly drove up the narrow road. At the top of the hill, they'd spotted a small ranch house set way back, not even visible from the road. Amador had backed up to the road and turned off the engine, then they retrieved their weapons from the back and went in on foot.

About ten yards away from the house was a small garage. Carefully easing the sliding door open, they found a dusty but otherwise immaculate Cadillac Escalade inside, its license plate matching the one stolen earlier that day. The two men grinned at each other, then Heriberto whipped out his cell phone.

"Who are you calling?" Amador asked. "The deputy said he should be informed if we found anything."

Heriberto frowned. "That bastard doesn't pay my salary. Besides, he's always cruising around like he owns the town, yet we're the ones called in to do any dirty work for him. Remember that damn town fair we had to provide security for? Just think of the reward we could get if we bring this gringo in for the company."

Amador smiled and nodded. "Works for me."

Heriberto hit the speed dial. "Sir, we've found him." He gave quick directions to their location, then positioned his cell phone so Amador could hear the conversation as well.

De Cavallos was explicit in his instructions. "Don't go in by yourself. Wait until at least one other team is there, preferably two. Also, there is something else I hadn't told you—he has my son as a hostage."

Heriberto and Amador exchanged glances. If they could save the boss's son, they could probably name their own reward.

"I want you to wait for more people, then go in and kill the American agent. Take the girl alive, but eliminate her if she gets in the way. Above all, save my son."

"Si, senor!"

BOLAN'S EYES OPENED at the first vibration of the small plastic box on his chest. He picked it up and realized the second line of passive motion sensors had been set off, meaning potential hostiles were already inside the perimeter.

"Damn it." The reviews of the sensors he'd used in L.A. and here had said they registered humans fairly well, but sometimes had trouble with vehicles. That would make sense. Someone driving up hadn't tripped the first one set across the driveway, but had set off the second one near the garage.

Rising, he clipped the holstered Beretta to his belt at the small of his back, put on his night-vision goggles, then slipped out into the hallway. Kelly was stretched out on the couch, covered by a worn comforter. The shotgun was on the floor beside her. Bolan smiled at the forethought. He peeked in on Everado. As he'd figured, the thug was sound asleep in the chair, exhausted from the events of the evening. Bolan took a second to look more closely, not that he cared, but it wouldn't do to have his hostage die before he'd outlived his usefulness. Although the young man looked like he had been dragged over a mile of hard road, his breathing was strong and steady. Even when Bolan picked him up and moved him into the small closet in the south corner of the room, Everado didn't wake.

Walking back into the living room, Bolan knelt by the couch and carefully placed a hand over Kelly's mouth before shaking her shoulder. Her eyes flew open and she grabbed at his hand, trying to pull it free before recognizing him and relaxing. Her brow knit in a frown as she looked down at her silenced mouth.

"Sorry about that." Bolan put a finger to his lips as he removed his other hand. "We've got company. Take this—" he handed her the shotgun "—and hole up in the kitchen behind the countertop. If you hear someone come in, and they don't whistle as they do, shoot a couple rounds to keep their heads down, then get out the back door to the nearest road and over to the SUV near your house. Got it?"

She nodded as she took the shotgun, checked its load, and slowly racked the slide to prevent making any more noise than necessary to chamber a shell. Tossing off the blanket, she crept into the kitchen using only the moonlight coming in through the dingy living-room windows to guide her. Meanwhile, Bolan turned on his night vision. He made sure Kelly was secure before sneaking to the back door and looking through the window at the side for any movement. Seeing none, he drew his Beretta before reaching over and slowly turning the doorknob while standing to one side of the door. When it stopped, he pulled the door open just enough for him to slip outside, then closed it behind him.

The night air smelled of grass and dew, and the world around him was lit up in bright green. Bolan edged to the corner of the house, reviewing the layout of the property in his head. The problem with the whole area was that there was absolutely no cover apart from the buildings themselves. The landlord had mowed the grass so that it was only a couple inches tall, eliminating the option of approaching the enemy by crawling through the underbrush.

He cocked his head as he heard the engine of an oncoming car in the distance. It was hard to tell where it was originating from, but it stopped nearby. He listened for a few more seconds, and was rewarded by the faint noise of what was probably a car door closing. Reinforcements, no doubt, he thought. They were facing at least four, and possibly as many as eight armed men now. Bolan had a couple of tricks up his sleeve, but the odds were definitely against him unless he could catch the enemy completely by surprise for at least a few seconds.

His gaze went to the roof of the house as an idea came to him. *Over, under, around or through…* It would be the last thing they would expect, and would give him a valuable vantage point. Plus, if the hitters were shooting at the roof instead of the house itself, it lessened the chances of Kelly or Everado getting hit by a stray bullet.

A black, cast-iron railing ran along one side of the concrete steps leading to the ground. Testing it, Bolan thought it would hold his weight long enough to reach the roof. Holstering his pistol, he climbed up, balancing on the railing and steadying himself with a hand on the wall. Gauging the distance, he jumped up and grabbed the corner, his fingers scraping on the shingles. Gritting his teeth, Bolan pulled himself up, supporting all of his weight on his arms. Although he was in top physical condition, it had also been a long day. Muscles creaking, he raised himself up far enough to throw a leg over and roll onto the rooftop.

Breathing slowly, he paused to see if his ascent had been noticed. Hearing nothing, he crawled to the peak of the gently sloping roof and looked down at the driveway, turning on the thermal aspect of his goggles as he did so to receive a combination of heat and night vision—the best of both worlds. He could now see over the small hill to the road, and spotted the two Escalades pulled off to one side, their cooling red-orange engines a pair of bright beacons in the night. Bolan also saw a cluster of heat signatures on the driveway approaching the house. There were six of them again, and as he watched, three split off to circle around the back, and the other three headed toward the front door. It's what I would do in their situation, he mused.

The moment the trio reached the top of the hill, they stopped for a whispered conference, then split up, one going left, one going right and the third going up the middle. Pros—they've been trained, probably in the Mexican military, he thought. Their coordination as they moved meant they had lines of communication, and the ease with which they navigated meant they were also wearing night vision, but apparently they still hadn't spotted him.

Bolan removed his last pair of flash-bang grenades from his side pocket, holding one in each hand. Dividing his attention between both approaching parties while trying to remain out of sight wasn't easy, but so far he was doing all right—after all, no bullets were flying yet. Both groups were less than ten yards away when he pulled the pins on the grenades. When they were within five yards of both doors, he tossed one bomb down in front and one in back, then lay down, closed his eyes and covered his ears.

The flash-bangs went off three seconds later, the brilliant pulses of light illuminating the night, accompanied by the loud reports that would deafen anyone within a ten-yard radius. The noise and light show died away, replaced by shouts and curses. Bolan rose to his feet and hit the back door party first—he didn't want Kelly stumbling out into them. Coming down enough to see over the edge, he spotted the three men stumbling away from the door, having ripped off their night vision, and two clapping their hands to their bleeding ears. Sighting carefully, Bolan's Beretta chugged softly six times. He took out one, but the other two men didn't fall. Instead they turned and started spraying fire wildly at the roof. Fortunately, Bolan was already climbing down and landed in the dirt next to the concrete steps, tucking and rolling forward. As the still-befuddled gunmen tried to sight on him, he took each one out with a head shot.

A shotgun's boom shattered the night, followed by several pistol shots from the front. Bolan leaped up the steps and into the back, pushing open the door while whistling as he hit the floor.

The shotgun roared again as he came in, but no pellets slammed into the faux wood above his head. Instead, someone out front began screaming at the top of his lungs. At the other end of the living room, Bolan saw the front door fly open and immediately triggered three shots at the person coming through, making them stumble backward. Bolan scooted over to Kelly, who was crouched behind the cheap countertop. "You okay?"

"Yeah—what the hell's with these guys? I gave them a full load and it didn't stop 'em!"

"They're wearing bullet-resistant vests. Come on, we're going out the back."

"What about Everado?"

"I'll get him." Bolan listened for a moment, but didn't hear any noise coming from the other bedroom. "Assuming he's still alive. Give me that."

Kelly handed over the shotgun, and Bolan emptied the magazine at the front door, then gave it back to her. "Keep this with you. Get near the back door and wait thirty seconds. If I'm not there, get out and get to the Caddy. Go!"

She ran for the back door, while Bolan headed through the living room, Beretta in hand. He ran past the front door, which was now perforated by buckshot and bullets, and hit the bedroom to see Everado half out of the closet, overturned on the ground, trying to inch his way toward the door.

"You aren't going anywhere just yet." The only window in the bedroom was toward the ceiling. Bolan drew his double-edged dagger and cut the young man's feet loose.

"Hey, how am I supposed to run like this?" he asked while Bolan smashed out the window with the butt of his pistol. Turning back, he cut the kid's hands loose as well.

"Jump. Try to run when you hit the ground, and I'll break both your arms."

Massaging his hands and wrists, Everado clambered out the window and half jumped, half fell to the ground. Bolan was right behind him, rising just as he started to make a break for the field. The sound of a shotgun slide racking stopped him in his tracks.

Kelly popped up from behind a huge natural gas tank. "I assume he's coming with us?"

"Do you think I would have risked my life to save his

if he wasn't? Let's go, tough guy." Bolan prodded Everado ahead of him as the three trotted to the far corner of the house. Behind them, they heard movement and more gunfire coming from the front as the remaining men stormed inside. Kelly rounded the corner, with Bolan coming up behind her. He hauled her back just as she was about to take off. "Hold up!"

"What? We gotta get out of here, right?"

"When I say."

Keeping one hand on Everado's shirt collar, Bolan edged close to the corner and peeked out. "You, keep your mouth shut. One peep and you'll be missing teeth."

Seeing no one there, Bolan motioned Kelly forward. "Run to the garage as fast as you can."

"Don't worry about me." Kelly took off like she was in the Olympics. No gunfire followed her progress, and she was able to open the door and slip inside.

"Okay, now you and me." Bolan shoved the kid ahead of him, keeping him moving forward while he watched the house, pistol ready in case the others showed themselves. Sure enough, he saw movement at the kitchen window, and fired four shots through the glass, causing shouts from inside. Scattered gunfire came from the door and window, but the bullets came nowhere near them. Bolan and Everado reached the garage door and got inside, closing the door just as headlights lit up the driveway and yard from an approaching vehicle.

"Time to go." Bolan shoved Everado into the SUV, where Kelly kept an eye on him. He inserted the key and turned it, but nothing happened. He tried again, with the same result.

"Watch him." Hitting the hood release, Bolan got out, noticing the dome light wasn't going on, and went to the front of the Escalade. Opening it, the hood light revealed a mass of cut wires. "Damn."

He walked back to Kelly and Everado. "We're not driving out in this thing, that's for sure."

Just then they heard an amplified voice. "Matt Cooper, this is the sheriff's department. We have you surrounded! You have thirty seconds to lay down your weapons and come out with your hands up, or we're coming in after you!"

12

When he heard the deputy's voice outside, Everado's expression turned from fear to confidence. "You hear that, *pendejo?* Better do what he says. Maybe my father will only kill you quickly instead of torturing you."

Bolan put the muzzle of his Beretta on Everado's forehead. "If it's hopeless, then why should I keep you alive any longer?"

"Hey, Cooper, now don't do anything you'll regret—"

"Take your own advice and shut the hell up. Those guys outside won't do a thing while I've got you." Bolan turned to Kelly, who had been rummaging in the backseat, coming up with the box of shells for the shotgun. She started pushing shells into the chamber as Everado stared in disbelief.

"It wasn't loaded? Son of a bitch—"

"Keep him quiet." Bolan grabbed another zip-tie from the glove compartment. "In fact, put your hands out." After securing the thug's wrists, Bolan flipped on his night vision and looked around the small utility shed. It was barely wide enough to open the doors of the SUV, and there wasn't much in there to use. Old, rusty tools lay on shelves mounted on the walls, and what looked like a gas can and a bunch of greasy rags were piled in the corner. He walked closer to the door. "Quintanar. You listening?"

"Yeah, Cooper. Why don't you surrender so we can help each other out?"

"I don't think I'd like the kind of help you have in mind. I still have Everado De Cavallos in here, and don't think I won't put a bullet in his head if I have to."

"Threatening him won't get you out of this."

"Maybe not, but it'll make sure none of your hired guns try anything stupid. Remember that the next time you try to give me an arbitrary deadline."

"There's no way out, Cooper. Give yourself up, turn Everado over to us and I'll do what I can for you."

"What would that be, a bullet in the back of the head instead of a tire filled with gas around my neck? No thanks, I'll take my chances."

Quintanar kept talking, but Bolan wasn't listening. Grabbing the gas can and rags, he walked back to the small window in the garage and peered out. As he'd suspected, there was no one outside—yet. "We're getting out of here. Keep an eye on him."

Dropping to the ground, he located the Escalade's gas tank and punctured it with his dagger, working the blade around to ensure the liquid flowed out steadily. He was also careful not to get any on himself. Scooting back out, he opened the lid to the tank, took out the cap and used a long screwdriver to force open the spring-loaded safety valve inside, stuffing another rag deep into the tube. The smell of gas filled the room as Bolan knelt and began shoving another rag into the gas can.

"Kelly, break out that window as quietly as you can. Everado, don't move a muscle." Bolan bunched the rest of the rags around the can as a makeshift fuse, tying one to the rag sticking out of the nozzle, then lit one of the rags on the floor using a fire starter and his dagger. The cloth smoldered and then flickered into flame, giving off the smoke he was hoping for.

"Dude, what the fuck! You're gonna kill us all!" Everado said from the corner.

"Not yet, genius. The gas fumes haven't filled the space yet, but they will in about thirty seconds." By then thick gray smoke had obscured the entire front of the garage. Deputy Quintanar was saying something outside, but no one was paying attention.

Bolan lit the rag in the gas tank and jogged to the back of the garage, scanning the field outside for gunmen. "Okay, we're leaving. I'm first, Everado second, Kelly's last." With one last look at the empty field, Bolan grabbed the top of the window and swung his legs through the hole, then squeezed his shoulders through and wriggled out, landing on the ground with his Beretta ready.

He heard a loud whump as the can near the door exploded, just as Everado got his upper body out of the window. "Hurry up!" Bolan grabbed him with his free hand and hauled him out, dumping him to the ground.

"Hey!"

"You're lucky I didn't drop you on your head." Bolan grabbed the shotgun from Kelly and helped her out. "Run like hell." He grabbed Everado and kept hold of him as they ran into the field. "Cut right after a hundred yards."

They hadn't gone more than a dozen steps when the Escalade exploded. Bolan heard a loud crash almost right after, and figured the front door had been blown off. A huge cloud of black smoke rose from the garage, which now had flames licking out from under its roof. Bolan heard frantic shouts from the other side of the building.

"Run faster, we're visible now. Follow me." Bolan led Kelly and Everado out another fifty yards, then circled back around the house to where the bodies of the three gunmen lay. "Kelly, search them for keys."

Grimacing, she did what he asked, finding a set on the second one. "How're we gonna reach their cars?"

"I'll handle that. You take Everado and cut west across those fields. Stop at the first road you come across and find a place to hide. I'll meet you on it." Bolan stared at Everado hard. "You listen to me very carefully. Any order she gives you, you do it immediately, because if you don't, I'll find you, and I'll kill you. Do you understand?"

The young man nodded, his Adam's apple spasming as he gulped with fear. Bolan pointed toward the road. "If I'm not there in ten minutes, or you see another vehicle approaching, take off. Get moving." Without waiting for a reply, the Executioner headed for the other corner of the house.

Flipping up his night vision, Bolan peeked out at the men running around in front of the garage, by then engulfed in flames. Quintanar was directing them to find water to put it out. Other men were busy stomping on embers that were floating into the nearby fields. Bolan grinned. He hadn't counted on that kind of distraction, but he'd take what he could get. Everyone's attention was still focused on the fire, making it easy for him to slip into the darkness.

As he'd hoped, there were no guards posted around the vehicles on the road. After matching the keys to the right vehicle, Bolan took a moment to flatten two tires on the other Escalade, then got into his new ride and drove off without headlights. At the first intersection he turned left and drove slowly down the road until he spotted two figures crouching in the ditch on the side of the road. He found Kelly guarding a sulking Everado, who was now sporting a black-and-blue mouse under his right eye.

"What happened?"

"He got stupid and tried to grab the shotgun. Got the butt in his face for his trouble."

"That true?" Bolan asked Everado. "Just for that, you get your feet tied as well. Get in."

With Everado in the backseat, Bolan took off the young man's cowboy boots and zip-tied his ankles together. "Ow, man that fuckin' hurts!"

"It's supposed to." Bolan cut the tie around his wrists.

"Thanks." Everado's smile faded when he saw Kelly hand Bolan another one.

"Hands behind your back."

"Aw, look man, I ain't gonna try anythin'—"

"Hands behind your back, or so help me I'll dislocate your shoulders and put them back there myself."

The young man put his hands in position, and Bolan promptly secured them. He got back into the driver's seat and headed the vehicle down the road.

Kelly watched him from the passenger's seat. "What next?"

"We've been lucky so far, but that can't last. Sooner or later De Cavallos is going to realize he has a lot more hostages than I do, and he's going to use them. I need to get you and him somewhere safe, and I also need to talk to someone in charge in town—someone who won't believe the lies that are being spread about me, and who I can trust to do the right thing. Do you know anyone like that?"

"Yup."

"Who, the mayor, or someone on the city council?"

Kelly shook her head. "Nope. Just follow my directions, and I'll take you right to him."

Rojas Quintanar had seen many American and Mexican comedy shows where an inept, bumbling police officer, thwarted by whatever ridiculous plan the heroic vigilantes or outlaws pulled off, would take his hat off and throw it on the ground in anger and disgust. He'd always laughed at the old joke, no matter how many times he'd seen it.

At this moment, however, he knew exactly how all of those officers felt.

He'd arrived in the middle of the firefight, despite radioing ahead the moment he'd been notified and telling the men to stay put until he'd arrived. Once the standoff was going on, he didn't have enough men to actually surround the garage, and had been trying to keep them in there until reinforcements arrived.

Then the building had caught fire, followed shortly afterward by the SUV inside exploding. They'd prevented the flames from spreading to the nearby fields, but it had been a close call, with large burned patches of grass around the ruined building and charred remains of the vehicle. When Quintanar had the place hosed down enough to get inside, he found no bodies, which he'd already expected. Immediately he swept and cleared the house, knowing he'd find it empty, too. When he did a head count of the men, he found three were missing and discovered their bodies behind the house. That was in addition to the two wounded men from the first team that had found Cooper's hideout. Finally, adding insult to serious injury, he'd sent the lone uninjured man back to bring an Escalade up to transport the wounded, only to find out that one of the SUVs on the road had been stolen and the other disabled.

It was enough to make a man weep. Instead, Quintanar called De Cavallos to fill him in on what had happened. His boss had not been pleased.

"Let me get this straight, Deputy. Once again you had this Cooper pinned down, and yet he managed to get away, killing even more of my men and still keeping my son as a hostage in the process. Is that correct?"

"Yes, sir, however, if the Cristobal men had followed orders and not moved in until I could have overseen—"

"If they had waited, my son might be dead right now. The only thing that is saving all of you is the fact that he is still alive, as far as we know."

There was no way for Quintanar to reply without earning a shallow grave. "Yes, sir. What would you have us do now?"

"I think we have been approaching this problem from the wrong direction. I am sending an order to recall everyone to the Cristobal factory. We are going to show this town exactly what we are capable of when someone crosses us. You should make arrangements to move your brother out of the hospital as soon as possible."

"Yes, sir. I'll take care of it. I can also bring with me a person that Cooper met in town—the editor of the paper, Casey Hinder."

"Excellent. He likes to take hostages, we can certainly do the same. She has a daughter, yes?"

"Yes, she does."

"Good, collect her, as well, and let me know once you have both of them in custody. It is very disappointing that the town of Quincyville has not been able to help us bring this man to justice. They are about to learn what happens when they do not follow the rules."

13

Bolan stared in disbelief at the building they'd pulled up to. "Here? This is where I'm going to find the person I need."

In front of him, the bright neon and gleaming chrome of Rollins's Diner shone through the windshield. A small light gleamed through the front windows from the back of the building. Bolan glanced at Kelly with a frown, hoping she wasn't playing some kind of joke.

Kelly rolled her eyes. "Where's the best place to eat in the county? Who's the man who knows everybody because they come in here all the time? Trust me, everyone from the mayor on down eats here. My dad…my dad used to come in every Friday for lunch, rain, shine, or tornado. If you need someone to help you with anything regarding this town, Brian Rollins is your guy."

Bolan checked his watch—5:30 a.m. De Cavallos had about one more hour to vacate the county, not that Bolan really expected him to give in to the demand. It had been a tactic to keep the other man off balance, as was taking his son as a hostage. But the longer he held Everado, the more dangerous the young man became for him. Sooner or later his father would do whatever it took to get his son back, and that could have disastrous repercussions on Quincyville itself. Bolan had to do all he could to prevent that.

He drove around to the back and parked. "I hope you know what you're doing."

"Didn't you say you needed someone who would take you at face value? Well, just sit down with him and talk for five minutes, and I'm sure you'll get him on your side. C'mon."

Bolan got out and hauled a dozing Everado with him as they headed to the door. The smell of cooking food filled the air, making Bolan's stomach rumble as he realized he hadn't eaten since the last time he was here.

Kelly banged on the service door, waited ten seconds, then banged on it harder.

"Hold on, hold on, I'm comin', damn it!" a voice shouted from inside. A few seconds later the heavy steel door cracked open, and a man Bolan recognized as the cook from yesterday poked his head out. "Kelly? Kelly Bitterman? Girl, what the hell you doin' bustin' my door down at five in the morn…" His voice trailed off as he noticed Bolan standing behind her—and Everado next to him.

Bolan gave him credit. He didn't gape or appear shocked, he just blinked twice as he looked the three up and down. "You must be Mr. Cooper?"

"That's right."

"According to the radio, you're cutting a wide trail of destruction through our fair town, including kidnapping young Kelly here."

"That's not what's going on—" Kelly started to say, but was hushed by Rollins.

"Hold on, girl, let the man speak for himself."

Bolan tried to sort out where to begin. "It's a very complicated story, Mr. Rollins, but the short end is that I'm a Department of Justice agent who's stumbled onto the biggest methamphetamine lab in the United States, operating right here in your town. I have one witness—" he nodded at Kelly "—who can testify that a sheriff's deputy working with these drug traffickers killed her parents, and the son of the head of security at Cristobal—" he shoved Everado forward "—who told me everything I need to know about what they're really manufacturing at the plant outside of town. I'd be happy to share everything I've found out with you if you'd like."

"Department of Justice, huh? I don't suppose you have any ID?"

"Yeah." Bolan produced the billfold and handed it over.

Rollins scrutinized it for almost a minute before handing it back. He looked at Kelly. "Is what he's saying the truth?"

"I can't vouch for the whole meth lab thing, but I saw Rojas Quintanar kill my mother." Kelly's voice shook a bit, but she retained her composure. "Since then, Everado has tried to capture us, and we've been on the run from both the Quintanar deputies and Cristobal's private security goons all night long."

Rollins rubbed his eyes. "Well, that's good enough for a start. Come on inside. I'll put young Mr. Everado on ice for the time being, and the three of us'll have a chat." He looked both of them up and down. "I'll bet you're both starved anyway."

TWENTY MINUTES LATER, Bolan polished off the last bite of what had to be the best pair of burgers he'd ever had. Kelly had wolfed down a huge bowl of chili with melted cheese and onions, followed by a slab of fresh-baked cherry pie with ice cream. She was lying down in one of the booths while Bolan and Rollins talked. He'd already filled in the cook on what had happened after he'd left the diner yesterday, and was listening as Rollins finished answering his question about whether he had ever served.

"Serving under Commander Franks as part of the VII Armor Corps in the Gulf was one of the finest things I've ever done in my life. After finishing my tour, I came back here to take over the diner from my father and start a family, and I've been here ever since." Rollins fixed Bolan with a steady stare. "And I've never cared much for the idea of these guys coming in and thinking they can tell us what they can and can't do in our town."

"From what I saw yesterday afternoon, you're not the only one who feels that way."

Rollins nodded. "I didn't get a chance to thank you for putting that snot-nose Everado in his place—it's been a long time coming. I only wish some of us'd had the guts to do it before now. Looks like we're about to reap what we sowed, aren't we?"

Bolan didn't drop his gaze. "I'm hoping to head that off before anyone else gets hurt, if possible."

Rollins leaned back in his booth seat and shrugged. "May be too late for that. You know, a lot of people thought Cristobal would be just what this town needed to survive at first, myself included, to be honest. As much as we wanted to preserve our way of life out here, we also realized it wasn't going to be possible without help from someone else. But look what that got us."

"It wasn't anybody's fault that Cristobal is what it is. From what I can tell, their company has a nearly airtight cover. I hate to say it, but even the U.S. government doesn't seem to have any idea that a major meth manufacturer and distributor is working under its very nose in the heartland of America. And if I hadn't taken a small detour out here yesterday, they still wouldn't know about it."

"So you've been in contact with the DOJ and DEA, right? They're going to investigate further? More important, if shit's about to go down, when are the reinforcements arriving?"

Bolan tried to keep a grimace off his face as he replied. "They probably will, but by the time they get out here in sufficient force, Cristobal will have either cleaned up its act and will only be producing legal pharmaceuticals, or they'll pack up and skip out, most likely extracting some kind of revenge on the town before they leave."

Rollins folded his arms across his chest and frowned. "On us? What for? Looking at it objectively, it's not like we asked you to come in here and poke around."

"Looking at it objectively, if you were the head of security for a company running a major illegal drug operation, and you received word that a U.S. government agent just happened to appear in town and started looking around recently, wouldn't you think someone had dropped a dime to bring him here? I don't think these guys are going to accept any pleas of innocence on your part—that's not how they do business."

"So you think we're in for it no matter what?" Rollins asked.

Bolan simply nodded.

"But they can't just destroy an entire town in the middle of America! Who'd stand for it?"

"They already have the police under their thumb. With a large enough group of armed men, they could destroy Main Street, burn the rest of the town and be well on the way to the Mexican border before any kind of force could be mobilized to stop them. In fact, if a cartel is behind this, it would be a great PR boost for them—'look what we did to a town in the middle of America, and got away with it.'"

Rollins leaned forward. "Over my dead body."

"Hopefully it won't come to that. I think De Cavallos is preparing a show of force to try and get you all to give me up to him. I've got an idea to beat him to the punch, so to speak, but I'll need help. Specifically, every man and woman who wants to stand up for their town and what they believe in. Normally I wouldn't bring civilians into a situation like this, but—"

"Seems like we're right in the middle as it is, and from what you've told me, it's gone too far already. A lot of people, including the editor of the town newspaper, have suspected there's more going on there than simple drug research and manufacturing, but no one could ever get anything concrete out of them. And anyone who came close was either warned off or disappeared."

"Disappeared or killed? Do you think that's what happened to the Bittermans?"

Rollins checked to see if Kelly was still sleeping before he replied. "Hard to say. Jack always was an opportunistic SOB, but he also loved this town, or at least he seemed to. If they were up to anything illegal, I'd like to say he would have turned them in, but I can't be entirely sure I'd be right."

"Well, now you're getting the chance to make your own choice."

"That's easy—I'm in. What did you have in mind?"

Bolan outlined his plan, which was fairly simple. The bulk of it involved getting people informed and organized. "Ideally, if we can get enough people in one place, the show of solidarity should convince these guys of the futility of trying anything further. What do you think?"

"I can contact three people on the Chamber of Commerce, each one a veteran, in five minutes. From there they can each contact three other people, who will do the same. It'll be an old-fashioned telephone tree. If I can't get you at least one hundred people willing to show up, then this town deserves to go up in flames."

Bolan smiled. "From what Kelly said, if anyone could pull this off, you could."

"I'll do whatever I can. What are you going to be up to in the meantime?"

Bolan's expression turned grim. "I'm going to be getting the evidence needed to prove these guys are running meth out of your town. We'll need it for the rest of the feds in case things go south. What's the best number to reach you at?"

Rollins gave him a cell phone number, and Bolan returned

the favor with Everado's cell number. "Don't call me unless it's an absolute emergency. Most likely I'll be in touch with you first. You know how to text?"

Rollins nodded. "I've raised three boys, the younger two are thirteen and fifteen. Believe me, I know more than I ever wanted to about it."

Bolan was busy changing his cell phone's ring feature to vibrate. "When you have as many people assembled as you think you can get, and if I'm not back or you haven't heard from me yet, text me. We'll go from there."

Rollins got up from his seat. "Then I'd better get busy." He headed to the back of the store, already calling his first target. Bolan was dialing as well, and heard a familiar voice pick up.

"Striker, you better be on the other end of this line," Aaron Kurtzman said.

"Up awfully early, aren't you, Bear?"

"Who has time to sleep with you running around raising hell in middle America?"

"Hey, more broad-minded contacts would call it self-defense. By the way, we owe a man out here a new garage."

"Do I even want to know why?"

"Probably not. I don't want to give particulars over the phone, but we'll take care of it when I get back to the farm."

"Why do I get the feeling that isn't the only reason you called in? You're planning something, aren't you?"

"You know me too well. I've been on the defensive ever since I got to this town. It's time I mounted an offense. And before this is over, I'm going to get evidence showing that Cristobal is manufacturing and distributing methamphetamine on an incredible scale on the continental United States."

"Well, you may have to bring home a chemist or two for direct testimony."

"What, the son of the head of security doesn't count for anything?"

"He'd help, assuming he lives through this. By the way, Akira's been sifting through Cristobal's computer system since your last check in, and hasn't come up with anything. Like everything else we've found, on the surface they seem to be a clean company. Ditto for the late Mr. Bitterman. Whatever he was doing, he hid his tracks well too."

"Cristobal must keep the data of their illegal activities on a closed system. That works for me, since I was planning to pay a visit to their site anyway. Was he able to get plans of the site itself?" Bolan asked.

"Yes, if you can get to a computer, they've been posted for your review. Remember, since you're gathering evidence, it would be good to throw the DEA a bone on something like this if possible. A little goodwill in Washington, D.C., can go a long way."

"I'll bring you whatever I can."

"And try to leave the town in one piece, will ya?"

"That's the plan. I'll be in touch." Bolan disconnected, then placed another call, checking the current time as he waited for the man on the other end to answer.

"Mr. Cooper, I presume?"

"Mr. De Cavallos, you have approximately forty-eight minutes to—"

"Actually, Mr. Cooper, I would suggest that you listen to me. You have something I want, so I have taken something I think you will want. Listen closely."

There was an odd scuffling noise, then Bolan heard harsh, ragged breathing over the phone. "Mr. Cooper? This is Casey Hinder, from the newspaper. These men have my daughter, Mr. Cooper—they have my daughter!"

Bolan remained calm, although he was starting to see red. "So you're adding kidnapping to the list of charges pending against you."

"I simply borrowed a page from your own playbook. I propose a simple exchange, the Hinder ladies for my son. You bring him to the Cristobal compound and we'll—"

"Not a chance. If I decide to agree to exchange these people, we do it on public ground, in broad daylight. I think Main Street will serve as a good place. I'll call you in an hour with the details."

Bolan snapped the phone closed and stared out the window at the first glimmers of sunrise starting to creep over the horizon. Aware of eyes upon him, he turned back to see Kelly staring at him.

"What's going on?"

Bolan didn't mince words. "De Cavallos took Casey Hinder and her daughter hostage."

"What are you going to do?"

Bolan rose from the booth. "I'm going to get them back."

14

Twenty-five minutes later, Bolan was lying in dew-soaked grass two hundred yards from the perimeter of the Cristobal Pharmaceutical compound, scanning the site with night-vision binoculars.

Although he was doing an infiltration with minimum reconnaissance, he had two things going for him—the hour before sunrise was when most people, including security guards, were at their most relaxed, making a successful penetration more likcly.

The second thing in his favor is that this would be the absolute last thing de Cavallos or his people would expect.

There were still plenty of obstacles in his way, however, the first of which was the ten-foot-high, electrified cyclone fence topped with razor wire that ringed the property. If he had access to air support, he could have simply dropped in on the roof of one of the buildings and gained an access point there. If wishes were airplanes, he thought.

A loud growl from the south caught his attention, and Bolan moved his glasses over to see a tractor trailer coming up the road. The name on the side read Juarez Brothers Trucking. Bolan had a pretty good idea about its final destination, and also how he could use it. When he saw that the truck had a large flipper, or aerodynamic hood on top of the cab, he went for it.

Plotting an intercept course, he ran for the road, trying to reach the ditch before the truck got close enough for the driver to spot him. Hitting the ground fifty yards out, he crawled on his belly into the dry ravine just as the truck slowed to turn into the driveway, the driver pulling to a stop at the guardhouse to present his documentation.

Crouched at the side of the ditch nearest the road, Bolan waited while the guards checked the semi thoroughly, including using mirrors to scan the roof and the underside of the tractor and its trailer. He tensed, ready to move at the right time, knowing the next few seconds would mean success or failure.

Finishing their sweep, the two guards turned to walk to the front of the cab. The moment their backs were turned, Bolan checked traffic, then rose and ran for the back of the semi, making sure to stay lined up with the center of the trailer to avoid being seen by the driver or the guards. He reached the rear doors, and had just gotten one foot on the rear guard when the truck lurched forward as it began passing through the gate. Bolan scrambled up the back of the trailer as fast as he could. Just as the roof of the tower came into sight, he pulled himself on top of the semi and lay flat, panting as the truck drove into the compound. Crawling to the front of the trailer, he peered around to make sure no one was watching, then stepped across the small opening between the trailer and the semi itself, tucking his body into the black space inside the hollow flipper. The acrid smell of exhaust as it belched out the twin smokestacks stung his nose, and he stifled the urge to cough.

From his vantage point, he saw the upper halves of buildings and caught snatches of shouted conversations, but most importantly, he heard nothing that sounded like an alert or warning that he'd been spotted. He was in—next he just had to get inside the building. For that, he was going to need a better disguise, preferably something in a white lab coat with an accompanying key card to get through the door.

The semi rumbled around to the back of the building and the driver began maneuvering his trailer into a dock.

The driver's door swung open with a creak, and Bolan heard muffled clomps as the driver climbed down, greeting another person in rapid Spanish. Bolan knew enough of the language to keep up, but he was hard-pressed to follow their quick bursts of conversation. Peeking out, he saw two men standing near the semi's rear wheels, one in a white coat reviewing paperwork, the other in cowboy boots, jeans and a white T-shirt, with a sweat-stained cowboy hat pushed back in his head. The two finished their conversation and the lab-coated man pointed to another building across the parking lot. With a nod, the man wearing the cowboy hat ambled in that direction, while man in the lab coat, still reading paperwork, began walking back to the main building.

Bolan wouldn't have a better shot.

Giving the man a two-step head start, he checked left and right to make sure he wasn't about to emerge in plain view of another worker. The rest of the trailer dock was empty. Bolan eased himself onto the back of the semi and jumped down to the ground on the opposite side of the trailer. Jogging parallel to the man heading back to the building, he ducked and crossed underneath the trailer, dodging around the large spare tire in its holder to see the backs of the man's legs as he walked on. It looked like he was about to head away from the trailer toward a concrete stairway leading into the building.

Glancing around one last time to make sure no one was nearby, Bolan drew his Beretta as he stepped out from under the trailer. Closing the distance between him and the employee in two large steps, he slammed the gun's butt on the back of the man's neck, knocking him unconscious.

Grabbing both him and his clipboard before he could fall over, Bolan dragged the guy back under the trailer.

His victim had everything Bolan needed—the white lab coat, a clipboard with papers on it and an identification badge that looked like it could get him inside. As he dressed, Bolan was mildly concerned about mixing with so many Hispanics, but he also knew that half of pulling off a successful infiltration was simply looking like you belonged wherever you were. The lab coat's sleeves were a bit short, but Bolan was counting on the ubiquitous jacket to turn him into just one more company man.

Leaving the unconscious man tucked between the wheels, Bolan pretended to read the paperwork on the clipboard as he left the dock area and headed around the building. He scanned along the side and spotted a door about a third of the way down. From his quick memorization of the building plans, this entrance should take him into the warehouse section of the building, where Cristobal stored large quantities of basic chemicals used in their procedures. Given enough time, Bolan thought he could find something that would produce a suitable bang in the area, but he had to find Casey Hinder and her daughter first before he could turn to sabotage.

Approaching the entrance, he ran the ID card through the slot next to the locked door, and was gratified to hear the click of it opening. He slipped inside, and as expected found himself in a large loading area with tall shelves filled with various supplies. Forklifts and men in lab coats similar to the one he wore were everywhere, filling orders, shouting commands and directing the flow of materials, but no one gave Bolan a second glance. Locating a door on the far wall to his left, the soldier walked unhurriedly to it. This one didn't have a card slot, so he just pushed through it.

The din of the loading area subsided to a dull roar. Bolan found himself in a quiet hallway with a row of thick glass windows on the far wall. On the other side was another large room that looked like a laboratory, with men and women clad entirely in one-piece white suits from head to two, wearing full-face masks and respirators. They were making a huge batch of something, although Bolan couldn't tell if it was meth.

Remembering the floor plans, Bolan decided to head to the front of the building. Since it was unlikely that Cristobal had any kind of detention facility, Casey and her daughter were more likely to be held in some kind of improvised room—a storeroom, for example, or perhaps a converted office. The only problem was finding it in the more than 150,000-square-foot facility without being discovered first.

Keeping his eyes on the clipboard, he proceeded down the hallway. He passed several more doors on his left, all of them made of metal and thick glass, with keypads and signs warning of biohazardous material and stating that all personnel should take appropriate safety precautions before entering the laboratory. One door opened as he passed, with three white-suited people emerging. Bolan didn't give them a second glance, and they didn't acknowledge his presence, either.

The hallway ended in another set of double doors. Without breaking stride, he pushed through, still pretending to be engrossed in his paperwork. A quick glance around revealed that he was in some kind of entrance hall, with at least two dozen people coming and going, each intent on his or her own task. At the far end was a bank of elevators that was constantly in motion, with a steadily moving line of people in front of it. A high wooden counter on the far wall in front of the main entrance doors was manned, but the two people behind it didn't seem to be interacting with anyone in the room. Bolan felt his frustration rising. Without some kind of guidance, he had no way of finding Casey and her daughter. It looked like he would have to ask for some assistance.

He walked toward the elevators, acutely aware that he was at least four to six inches taller than everyone else in the large room. Still, no one seemed to give him a second glance. Joining the elevator line, Bolan shuffled forward with the rest until he was packed onto a clean, sterile-smelling car with the others. People got off and on at various floors—there were five, he noted—and by the time he reached the top of the building, there was one other person with him, another lab guy with tousled blond hair and a distracted air who was constantly texting on a smartphone. Bolan thought about interrogating him but decided against it. The guy was probably too wrapped up in whatever he was working on to notice any prisoners, much less women, being brought into the building.

The elevator dinged their arrival, and Bolan let the other man leave ahead of him. The foyer outside was tiled in marble, but the double doors to his right were hardwood and attended by a gray-suited man who was obviously a security guard.

Bolan's interest increased. Anywhere people weren't supposed to go usually meant that was where the company was keeping things—or people—it didn't want others to have access to. What better place to start looking?

He followed the scientist to the door, where they were blocked by a guard named Hernando, as his name tag indicated. The man walked up and presented his badge, which the guard scanned with a hand reader. Apparently he checked out, because the door opened, and he walked through. Bolan caught a glimpse of plush carpeting and walls covered in dark cherrywood.

Bolan tried to bluff his way through by following the first man, but the guard stopped him with a hand on his chest. "ID badge, please."

"Oh, sure—sorry." Bolan handed it over. The guard scanned it and read the output on his small screen with a frown.

"You're not cleared for access to this level. Where are you—" The guard's question trailed off as he looked closer at the ID card, seeing no resemblance between the picture and the man standing in front of him. He reached for the microphone on his shoulder, but Bolan stopped him with a gentle poke.

"Don't touch that." He shifted his clipboard to the side enough for the guard to see, but not for any overhead cameras to spot what was happening.

The guard looked down to see the silenced muzzle of a Beretta 93-R pressed into his stomach. He took a sudden breath and started to raise his hands.

"No, no—keep them at your sides. That's right, just act naturally." Bolan reached down and unplugged the guard's mike from the walkie-talkie on his belt. He also slipped the man's canister of pepper spray from its clip and put it in his own pocket. "Try anything stupid, and I will gut-shoot you and leave you here to die."

"Who are you? What the hell do you want?"

Bolan kept his ear open for the elevator behind him. "De Cavallos brought two women here from town, and I'm here for them," he replied.

"I don't know what you're talking about—"

Bolan increased the pressure on the man's abdomen. "Then I guess I'll have to shoot you and leave you here to maybe get help eventually. You ever seen a gut-shot man? They bleed something awful, scream and cry while they bleed out slowly. Recovery takes weeks."

Beads of sweat popped out on the man's hairline. "Look, I got a wife and three kids at home—"

Bolan thumbed the hammer back on his pistol. "Hope they'll like visiting you in the hospital for the next few weeks. You either help me now or get used to eating through a tube."

"All right! All right! Those two aren't even in this building. They're being held in a smaller outbuilding elsewhere on the site. Looks like you came all the way up here for nothing."

"No problem." Bolan grabbed the guard's shoulder with his free hand. "You're going to take me to them."

"What? No way, I can't leave my post, I'll be canned for sure."

"Alive and unemployed is better than your widow collecting your last paycheck, wouldn't you agree, Hernando? Let's move."

He slipped behind the guard and prodded him toward the elevator. Hernando glanced back, sweat trickling down the side of his face. "You know they're going to investigate why I'm going without leave in about one minute, right?"

"Well, then, you better hope this elevator doesn't stop at every floor on the way down."

The elevator chimed, and the two men stared at the pair of chemists about to disembark. "Shouldn't there be a guard on duty up here at all times?"

Hernando remained silent until Bolan jabbed his kidney with the Beretta. "Uh, they're sending up a replacement in just a few minutes. I'm needed elsewhere in the building."

"Can't you just buzz us in now?"

"Sorry, we've got to go." Bolan shoved Hernando past the two men and hit the button for the ground floor. Their shocked looks were the last things he saw as the doors closed.

"Oh, man, you're in for it now. They're gonna make some calls, and you'll be screwed."

"Just remember—if you ever want to see your kids again, you get me out of here and to that building."

The guard had the balls to look put upon, even with a gun in his ribs. "Damn man, why me?"

"You were the first guard I came across, that's why."

"My lucky fucking day."

"You're doing fine so far. Remember, just act naturally as we head to the front doors and don't stop for anyone."

Luck was on Bolan's side this time. They got to the ground floor without anyone else getting on. The doors opened, and Bolan escorted his captive out of the elevator and across the room. As before, no one took much notice of the pair. At the front doors, Hernando made to swipe his card through the slot, but Bolan stopped him. "Nope, use mine."

With a resigned sigh, the guard did as he was told. The door clicked open. "Let me guess," Bolan hissed as he shoved the man through the door. "Using your card would have set off some kind of alarm because you aren't where you're supposed to be here, right?"

"Something like that. Can't blame a guy for trying."

"Your loyalty to your company when the alternative means severe, painful injury is admirable, to a point. You do know what they make here, don't you?"

"Yeah. I'm in security, not the janitorial staff. I'm not stupid, but the pay is good, and until you showed up, there wasn't much to do. No one was crazy enough to break in to this company."

"Yeah, I have a bad habit doing things my way." They made it to the corner of the huge building, and Bolan spotted a small house trailer with two men guarding the front door. He sighed. "Don't tell me they're being held in there."

"What tipped you off, the guards? Yeah, that's where they are."

"All right, keep those feet moving."

Hernando slowly started walking. "And what am I supposed to tell them when we get there? If they don't receive confirmation from De Cavallos about you going in, we're both dead."

"You let me worry about that." Bolan glanced around as they got closer. No one was nearby. Apparently security kept a wide perimeter around their guests.

"We are so not going to get away with this."

"Not with that attitude, we're not." By this point they were only a few yards away. Bolan took one last look around—still no one else in sight on this side of the building. "Engage the guard on the left. Tell him you have orders to relieve him."

Although the morning heat was rising fast, neither of the pair looked uncomfortable in the least. They both stood at parade rest, their eyes hidden behind mirrored sunglasses, their uniforms clean and pressed. Bolan's experienced gaze sized both up as professionals—a bluff wasn't going to get them far.

"Hey, Miguel! They want you inside, something about the alarm system on level three not working."

The man on the left regarded the two men through his shades. "Haven't heard anything about reporting back in. I'm gonna have to confirm it—"

The whoop of an alarm siren blared across the compound, making every head but Bolan's turn toward the large building. The guard on the right looked back at Hernando and the chemist in the ill-fitting lab coat and put it together first, his hand grabbing for his sidearm. Tossing the clipboard in the left man's face, Bolan raised his Beretta and shot the drawing guard through the right eye. As he started to collapse, the other man had just gotten the clipboard and papers out of his face when a 9 mm subsonic bullet shattered his forehead and burrowed deep into his brain.

"Thanks, Hernando." Bolan pistol-whipped the guard across the back of the head, sending him sprawling to the ground. The soldier leaped up the stairs and pounded on the door. "Casey, are you in there?" he shouted over the din of the alarm.

"Yes, who are you?"

"Department of Justice! Get as far back from the door as you can!" Bolan gave them a five count, then put several bullets into the aluminum around the knob. With a powerful kick, he smashed open the door and stepped inside.

The trailer was a former office, modified to serve as a temporary holding cell. The nearly bare space, containing only a battered metal desk and two flimsy folding chairs, was already roasting in the prairie heat, reeking of perspiration and urine. "Matt Cooper, I've come to get you out of here!"

"Oh, thank God!" Casey's dirty, sweat-streaked face appeared from behind the desk, followed by her daughter. "Department of Justice? I thought you were a journalist," Casey said with some confusion, but quickly realized this wasn't the time to worry about such details. "Who's with you, the FBI? Homeland Security?"

Bolan was already moving and was at the desk and taking her arm. "No, just me. We have to go, right now."

"Just you? But how do you expect to get out—"

"No time to explain. You'll have to trust me. Come on, we can't stay here." Guiding her to the door, Bolan kept her behind him as he checked the yard. Seeing no one coming so far, he pulled her out to the metal landing, checking to make sure that her daughter was following. "Can you handle a pistol?"

Casey nodded, then frowned. "Yes—wait, you mean like shoot someone?"

"More like just keep their heads down." Boland led the two down the stairs, where Casey sucked in a breath when she saw the two bodies.

"Oh God. You're serious, aren't you?"

Bolan had already stripped the guards of their pistols and

offered one, butt-first, to Casey. "It may make the difference between getting out and not."

She grabbed it and nodded at her daughter. "Connie can handle one, too. She's been shooting target since she was ten."

Bolan was already walking toward the back of the main building. "Normally I'd prefer not to—no offense—but we don't have much choice." He handed her another pistol, sticking the third one in his belt. "Remember, just keep their heads down. You won't have to aim at them."

"Daddy always said to never use a gun unless you plan to hit what you're aiming at," the girl said, holding the SIG-Sauer firmly with both hands.

"In that case, aim for the second floor of the building— you can't miss." The back wall of the massive structure seemed to stretch on forever, and Bolan was concerned that they would be caught in a cross fire or ambush before reaching their goal. He kept glancing back, expecting to hear shouts and gunfire from the trailer at any moment. Finally they got close to the corner. Bolan came to a stop a few feet away, motioning them to stay back. "Casey, watch behind us."

He eased up to the corner and peeked around. The semi was still there, but now the dock had a pair of guards on this side, and Bolan figured there was at least one more on the platform leading inside.

He ducked back. "Two guards on this side, probably at least one more on the other side. I'm going to try to take them. Be ready to go for the truck on my signal." He mussed up his hair and rubbed his sleeve in the dirt, then across his face. "Keep an eye out behind you as well."

Tucking his pistol under his lab coat, Bolan hunched over and staggered around the corner, groaning as if in pain.

"*¡Ayúdeme!*" he gasped as he stumbled toward the guards.

One of them went to help him, the other hit his lapel mike and began speaking into it.

Bolan reached out a hand to the nearer guard as if he was about to hold on to him for support. He did grab his arm, then brought out his Beretta and stuck it in the man's stomach, making sure to go underneath the bulky body armor he was wearing.

The guard had just enough time to look down and register what was about to happen when Bolan pulled the trigger twice. The bullets tore through his lower abdomen, mangling the small intestine and dropping the man to the ground. He clutched his middle, trying to suck in enough air to scream.

The other man was pulling his pistol while still talking into his walkie-talkie. Bolan yanked his gun free and brought it around, sighting on the man and firing a split second before he did. The guard's bullet whizzed by, cracking the air as it broke the sound barrier. Bolan's shot hit him in the collarbone, which did make him drop his pistol. Steadying his right hand with his left, Bolan put a second shot through the man's nose, killing him instantly.

Ducking, Bolan looked underneath the trailer for running boots. Seeing none, he looked back at Casey and her daughter. "Let's go!"

The two women ran behind him as Bolan headed toward the tractor trailer. Hopping up on the gas tank, he opened the passenger door and hustled both of them inside, then joined them, scrambling past into the driver's seat.

"Shit, no keys!" Casey had already checked both visors, hoping for a spare.

"Give me a minute. Keep watch out the driver's window!" Bolan was already wriggling beneath the steering column and used the butt of his pistol to crack open the plastic housing. Quickly isolating the correct wires, he drew his dagger and stripped the ends, then touched them together. The engine turned over, then rumbled to life, just as several shots were fired out of the driver's window.

"What's happening?" Bolan asked as he came back up and Casey scooted over into the passenger seat.

"Guards coming out the door. Put a few shots above their heads to keep 'em inside."

"All right, we're leaving anyway." Hitting the trailer release button, Bolan pressed the clutch, shifted into low and stepped on the gas while releasing the clutch. The semi lurched forward, and he quickly gave it more gas to prevent a stall. He heard a grinding noise, then a loud crash as the trailer broke loose and crashed to the ground.

Picking up speed, Bolan pulled out of the dock area and headed for the main gate. He had just pulled around the corner of the building when he was confronted by two Escalades coming right for him. Hitting the gas, Bolan picked up enough speed to shift into second gear and drove straight ahead. The pair of SUVs tried to swerve around him, but Bolan didn't want both coming after him.

"Hang on!" As they passed, he wrenched the wheel hard right, sending the bumper of the semi into the side of the Escalade. The heavy truck crunched into the rear quarter panel of the SUV, crumpling metal and sending a dagger of steel into the rear tire, which exploded under the pressure. Bolan saw the vehicle roll to a stop in a cloud of dust. He shifted again, picking up even more speed.

By then he was aligning the truck with the main gate, which had gone to full compound lockdown mode. However, they weren't really expecting a semi to come barreling at them. Scattered shots came at the truck, one bullet starring the right windshield but not hitting anyone inside. Bolan braced himself for return fire, but none came.

"Watch out for the road spikes!" Casey shouted.

Glancing at the road next to the guardhouse, Bolan spot-

ted the tire shredders that had just popped up. "No problem."
He aimed the truck a few degrees to the right.

"You're not going to—"

"You better get your daughter into the back." Bolan didn't
look at her as he adjusted his aim a bit, then braced for
impact. The guards tried to wave him off, then aimed their
pistols, but realized his intent and dived out of the way just
in time.

The semi hit the guard shack at fifty miles an hour, de-
molishing the small building in a shower of wood, shingles
and metal. Part of the roof slid onto the hood, until Bolan
juked the wheel hard enough to make it slide loose. He
checked his mirrors for pursuit, but the escape had been so
quick that the company hadn't mounted an effective group
to chase them. Even the untouched SUV wasn't coming after
them.

"Everyone okay?"

Casey's head stuck up from behind the passenger seat.
"Yeah, until Cristobal gets their act together and comes after
us. You got enough gas in this thing to get us to Canada?"

Bolan shook his head. "No one's running or hiding anymore. We're going to take care of this once and for all—right
here in Quincyville."

15

Fifteen minutes later, Bolan stood in the middle of a deserted Main Street, staring off to the south. The alarm siren at Cristobal had fallen silent a few minutes ago, and that was the signal he'd been waiting for.

His gaze flicking left and right along the empty street, devoid of cars or the slightest sign of other human life, he flipped open Everado's cell phone and hit the speed-dial button for the elder De Cavallos.

It was answered on the second ring. "You either possess incredible skills or unbelievable luck, Mr. Cooper."

"I just don't like innocent people getting in the middle of our business, Mr. De Cavallos."

"Are you saying that my son isn't innocent?"

"Anyone who tries to kidnap a Department of Justice agent is far from innocent," Bolan said.

"You are as much a DOJ agent as I am. No true agent would have done what you just did at my compound. Your government would never have allowed it."

"You learn fast. I did that to serve you fair warning. You have approximately twenty-five minutes to meet my deadline. You've already seen what I did to your security. If you don't go, I'm coming after you as well."

"I was in the process of wrapping things up here until our

perimeter was breached, which delayed the safe shutdown of our production lines. There are many dangerous chemicals on-site, and it would be a shame if, due to haste or improper storage procedures, a toxic cloud were to escape and contaminate the town."

Bolan heard the implied threat loud and clear. "That would be too bad, especially considering that your son would be at ground zero."

"Yes, that would be a shame. You've outmaneuvered me at every turn, Mr. Cooper. It seems that I have no choice but to acquiesce to your terms. I would, however, like to pick up my son before I leave."

"Fine. Come to Main Street in ten minutes. He and I will be waiting for you." Bolan snapped the phone closed, then flipped it open again and used the walkie-talkie feature to contact Rollins.

"How'd it go?" the man asked.

"About how I expected. De Cavallos is planning to roll into town and collect his son, then extract a big load of payback for my messing up his operation."

"Except we're not going to let that happen."

Bolan smiled at the determination he heard in the man's voice. "That's the spirit. I can't promise this'll go down without any collateral damage, but I'll do my damnedest to keep it to a minimum. Keep everyone in position and ready to go on my signal."

"Yeah, some are getting a touch overheated, but they'll all be ready to go when you give the word."

"Good. You sure your nephew won't get into any trouble with that 'requisition' he pulled from the armory?"

"Considering the commander of the Guard in this county is my brother, I don't think there'll be any trouble. They've already signed off on the paperwork that says they were on 'maneuvers' when they encountered the situation."

"Good. You all are taking enough risks here already."

"It's something we should have done a long time ago. You just opened our eyes to what was really going on here."

"I'm sure you would have handled it yourselves in time."

Rollins grunted. "Maybe. This town was like a lot like a hound dog lying on the porch with a nail poking it. As long as it didn't really start to hurt, we were all willing to put up with the occasional twinge of pain. Now, however, it appears that nail is about to get shoved somewhere deep."

"Not if I can help it," Bolan replied.

"Before all this gets underway, is there anything else you need?" Rollins asked.

Bolan looked around one last time and nodded. "Just the bait."

"We'll have that order of punk-on-ice out to you shortly."

"Thanks." Bolan cut the walkie-talkie feature and dialed Stony Man Farm. "Bear."

"Striker. Good to hear your voice this morning. I guess the fact that you're calling in means you haven't left that town yet."

"No. Our friends from south-of-the-border are pretty good poker players, but they haven't learned that I hardly ever bluff." Bolan filled him in on the conversation with De Cavallos, including the implied threat about the gas cloud. Kurtzman's reaction was typical.

"Damn it, Striker, Barbara and I had our hands full getting a strike force together that was close enough—which is inbound as we speak, which, by the way, was no small feat, I might add—and now you want me to somehow come up with a hazmat team that can handle a potential toxic gas cloud that might rival Bhopal?"

"Barbara" was Barbara Price, mission controller at Stony Man Farm. "Something like that. Look, I'm going to do everything in my power to ensure that nothing happens here, but you'd best have that team on standby, just in case."

"I just got the phone out of my ear for the first time in the past three hours, and now I gotta get back on it again. By the way, you don't even want to know what Hal thinks of all this."

Bolan couldn't help grinning at the image of Hal Brognola, one of his oldest friends and allies in his global fight against evil, chewing his unlit cigar as he tried to handle what was happening in America's heartland. "Just tell him it wasn't my fault—really."

"Oh no, I'm not even gonna try to justify this. You'll have plenty of time to tell him yourself when you get back."

Bolan spotted a pickup truck turning onto Main Street from the direction of Brian Rollins's diner. "Almost showtime, Bear, I gotta go."

"Give 'em hell, Striker."

"You know it." Bolan shut the phone and waited.

Twenty seconds later, a frost-covered and shivering Everado De Cavallos was driven up in the back of a pickup truck, watched by three members of the high-school football team. He was dumped over the side with little grace, and landed on his hands and knees in front of Bolan. In the driver's seat, Rollins nodded at Bolan before driving off again. In seconds the street was deserted except for the soldier and Everado.

"M-my f-f-father…will k-kill you…for this…" Everado said through chattering teeth.

"We'll just see about that, won't we?" Shading his eyes from the rising sun, Bolan looked south again. "You should probably just stay down there. It'll be safer for you."

Everado mustered enough nerve to spit on Bolan's shoe. "Fuck you, *cabron!*"

Bolan eyed his shoe, then wiped it off on Everado's torn, stained designer jeans. He didn't say a word and kept looking to the south.

Three minutes later, his patience was rewarded by the sight of a convoy of Escalades coming up the highway, escorted by something Bolan wasn't expecting. The steady thrum of a helicopter's blades beat the air as the aircraft flew above the SUVs coming into town.

Bolan got on the horn to Rollins. "You spot the air support?"

"Yeah. I shoulda told you about that, but we got it covered. Don't worry, they won't spoil the surprise."

"All right, get everyone ready, and above all, wait for my signal. It's going to happen in the next three minutes."

Bolan clicked the phone closed, put it in his pocket and waited. The helicopter flew past him, circling around the Main Street area, no doubt looking for hidden people or vehicles. Bolan hoped Rollins had concealed his people well. The entire plan depended on maintaining the element of surprise.

The Escalades, six in all, purred up the street. Two pulled past Bolan and took up positions a block away, stopping in a V-formation that blocked any traffic that might try to come in from the north. The trailing pair did the same at the south end of the street, cutting off access or escape on that end as well.

The main vehicle, an extended Escalade that Bolan noticed was heavily armored, rolled to a stop in the middle of the street, flanked on the right by the last SUV. As if choreographed, doors opened and men spilled from every one of the immaculate vehicles. Each was armed with a machine pistol or submachine gun, and they all took up positions watching Bolan from the cover of their car doors or behind the engine blocks of their Escalades.

Bolan watched the show without moving a muscle, his hands still at his sides, shoulders relaxed, feet about shoulder-width apart. After all, his efforts had ensured that they were missing at least nine men, including the injured deputy from the previous night. He had to be looking at pretty much everybody who was left in Cristobal's security force.

The helicopter passed by overhead, its racket shattering the stillness.

The front right passenger door of the extended Escalade opened, and a man who had to be De Cavallos stepped out. He was dressed in a cream-colored linen suit, its crisp lines accentuating his lean form. Hand-tooled cowboy boots with chiseled silver points on the toes adorned his feet. His black hair was immaculately styled, his eyes hidden behind mirrored sunglasses. Bolan watched him carefully as he took in the scene, with his son prone in front of the man who had been giving him so much trouble over the past day and night. He didn't react upon seeing the insulting sight, but simply glanced left and right before strolling toward Bolan. The two men who had gotten out of the vehicle before De Cavallos fell in behind him, weapons at the ready. Bolan noticed that one of the men was Deputy Rojas Quintanar, holding a sawed-off pump shotgun.

Bolan let them approach to within a few yards before prodding Everado with the toe of his boot. "Get up."

The young man rose to his feet, swaying unsteadily next to Bolan.

"That's far enough."

De Cavallos lowered his sunglasses to look at Bolan, then past him, then around at the rest of the street. "You are an incredibly bold man, Mr. Cooper. I cannot think of anyone in our respective lines of work who would be so daring as to meet me alone."

Bolan shrugged. "I have friends in high places."

De Cavallos frowned, as if trying to discern whether his words had a hidden meaning. When nothing changed in the barren landscape around them, he smiled. "That I find hard to believe. You've already confirmed that you're not with the government. No organization would ever sanction what you've done over the past twenty-four hours. Yet you are also not a mercenary, since you didn't seek to extort any kind of ransom or payment in exchange for you leaving me alone—a ransom, I might add, I would have gladly paid. In fact, given your skills, I would have been happy to have gotten a chance to hire you myself. Someone with your capabilities would have proved quite useful to our organization."

Bolan stared evenly at him, his ice-blue gaze boring into the man's deep brown eyes. "Unfortunately for you, I'm not for sale. Besides, I think I would have screwed up the interview anyway."

"So it would seem. A pity, that. Before we conclude our transaction, there is one thing I must know. Why did you do all of this? I cannot possibly see what gain there was for you..." De Cavallos's expression turned thoughtful, and he stroked his chin. "Unless you are one of that rarest of American citizens...the true patriot. Ready, able, and willing to risk his life in the pursuit of liberty, justice and the American way, is that not how the saying goes?"

The helicopter passed overhead again, the draft from its rotor blades kicking up dust on the street. Bolan allowed himself a tiny nod at the other man's words. "Something like that."

De Cavallos motioned his son to come to him. The younger De Cavallos slunk away like a beaten dog. His father grabbed him by the chin and lifted his face up to examine it, then released it, turning his attention back to Bolan. "People like you are a vanishing breed."

"I've heard that before. The funny thing is, there are more of us around than you might imagine."

Again De Cavallos glanced around at the empty street, the deserted stores. "Perhaps, but you seem to be the only one here. And in the next few seconds, America will have one less hero."

"I wouldn't be so sure of that." Bolan raised his left hand to emphasize his point, and the two men guarding De Cavallos aimed their weapons at him. The Executioner heard the actions of the other guns around him being readied, and then it happened.

On every rooftop of every building along the Main Street of Quincyville, men and women popped up, at least thirty on each side of the street, every one armed with a rifle that they pointed down at the men below. One of them reared up so fast that the black blanket he'd been hiding under slipped off and fell to the sidewalk below.

De Cavallos and his men looked around uncertainly as two pairs of camouflaged Humvees appeared from side streets on the far sides of the pair of Escalades at either end, blocking in the SUVs. Each vehicle had a pintle-mounted M-249 SAW machine gun mounted on it, manned by a helmeted soldier. In seconds, the cartel men had gone from being in complete control of the situation to being hopelessly outnumbered.

Despite the gravity of Bolan's situation—next to the drug runners, he was the most vulnerable, standing right in the thick of the huge Mexican standoff that had just developed—the Executioner still savored the look of disbelief and shock that appeared on De Cavallos's face.

"There's still plenty of Americans willing to stand up and fight for what they believe in, whether it's their country, their neighbors, or simply their way of life. And they're more than willing to stand up to scum like you, coming into our country to spread your drugs."

De Cavallos recovered fast, his expression changing from surprise to anger to resignation in the span of a few seconds. "Once again it seems that I have underestimated you, Mr. Cooper."

"Then you see the folly of trying to continue this confrontation, don't you, Mr. De Cavallos?"

The Mexican nodded. "I most certainly do, however, I'm not about to let myself be arrested and extradited back to my own country." He twitched his wrist, and suddenly he was holding a small black box in his right hand. "This is a radio-controlled detonator to the charges that have been planted in the Cristobal factory. The toxic cloud resulting from the mixing of the chemicals there would certainly wipe out this town and everyone in a one-hundred-mile radius."

Bolan kept his voice even as he replied, "Even you wouldn't destroy what had to cost the cartel millions of dollars to build." He felt dozens of eyes upon him from above, everyone waiting for one of two signals to be given—either stand down, or open fire.

De Cavallos's face hardened, and Bolan saw the true, ruthless drug dealer that lurked beneath his civilized veneer. "You will let us drive out of town unharmed, or else I will unleash a chemical nightmare upon your precious little town."

In answer, Bolan licked his finger and held it up as he turned slightly away from his opponent. "I'd be a lot more worried about that if the wind wasn't blowing south-southeast. The only people you'd catch in that cloud is yourselves. The next town is thirty miles to the east. There's only a hundred miles of empty prairie to the south."

That wasn't entirely true. If De Cavallos did unleash the chemicals, there still was a chance the town could be caught in the fallout. But Bolan's words had the desired effect. They made the other man pause as he also checked the direction the wind was blowing.

He returned his attention to the man in front of him. "Only one way to find out…"

But Bolan was already moving. His right hand, which had been slowly creeping up toward his belt, now flashed to the Beretta hidden under his jacket. Drawing it in a single fluid motion, he snap aimed and fired at the box in De Cavallos's hand. The 9 mm bullet exploded the box into a spray of plastic and electronics, slashing the man's hand open and making him shout in surprise and pain.

Bolan didn't stop to see what effect his shot had on the man, but moved his pistol ten degrees left and put a bullet right between Rojas Quintanar's eyes before the man could perfectly aim his rifle. As the deputy fell, Bolan sent two more bullets toward the second guard as he dived to the ground, knowing all hell was about to break loose around him. Rolling onto his back, he fired at the nearest guard's feet, more to make him take cover than in hopes of actually hitting him. But as he triggered his Beretta, he heard a sound that made his blood run cold.

The moment before everyone opened fire, the roof of the extended, armored Escalade split open to reveal a six-barreled minigun. It popped out and unloaded on the nearest building with an ear-splitting roar. The front of the shop disintegrated in a shower of glass and brick, making the townspeople on the roof duck for cover.

The M-249 SAWs on the Humvees opened up from both ends of the street, shredding the men running for cover either to or from the Escalades. One managed to get inside a vehicle and try to drive away, but sustained bursts of 5.56 mm rounds into the engine and tires brought him to a halt after only going a few yards.

Then it was as if the heavens had opened up, and lead poured from the sky instead of rain.

Bolan's calculated risk—that De Cavallos would surrender when faced with what should have been overwhelming odds—had gone terribly wrong. He ran for the nearest cover, which happened to be the underside of the armored Escalade. Its chain gun was still pouring a firestorm of destruction into the rooftops at a rate of 4,000 rounds per minute. The tops of the roofs were pulverized under the machine gun's onslaught. While it raked the left side of the street, the shooters on the opposite side tried to take it out by concentrating their fire, but the lighter rifle shells, even the .30-06 and .300 Winchester Magnum bullets, ricocheted off the body. Bolan thought about trying to contact Rollins, but wasn't sure the man would be able to hear him. The deafening thunder all around him was an almost physical force that battered at his ears and skull.

All around him, the gunmen on the ground dropped like flies, cut down by a variable hail of bullets. The Escalades at both ends of the street sagged on blown tires, their windows shattering, one hood flying up, only to be perforated by several more rounds. Thick clouds of burned cordite filled the street, its familiar, acrid odor filling Bolan's nose.

Then Bolan heard an even louder racket above the ear-splitting thunder of rifle fire as a shadow passed overhead. The helicopter came in low and out of the south, a pair of gunmen wielding M-16s shooting at the remaining riflemen on the roof. One of the M-249s swiveled and opened up as the helicopter approached, the 5.56 mm rounds spitting out to star the helicopter's windshield.

The pitch of the aircraft's engine changed suddenly, its smooth roar turning choppy. The aircraft's shadow began whirling around on the street as the pilot fought for control. Bolan watched the M-249 gunner pour more fire into the aircraft, then heard a small explosion. The chopper reared up, then accelerated right into a storefront, where its blades shattered into shards of deadly shrapnel flying in every direction. Bolan ducked behind a heavy-duty tire as he heard the thunks from pieces hitting the side of the SUV. What was left of the fuselage crashed to the ground about fifteen yards from Bolan's position. One man managed to stagger out of the crumpled, smoking wreck, only to be cut down in a hail of bullets. The chain gun above was still spraying out ragged bursts every few seconds, as if the gunner inside was picking his targets with more care.

The engine of the Escalade started, and Bolan flattened himself against the ground as the SUV lurched backward. Although both front tires had been shot several times, that didn't seem to impede the driver's handling of the big vehicle. Bolan was left lying in the middle of the road, as the Escalade barreled into the two wrecked Escalades to the south, shoving the bullet-ridden hulks aside as if they were toys. One of the Humvees tried to challenge it, while the other one backed away. The M-249 opened up on the approaching SUV, which gained speed as it backed up.

Then its cannon finally finished its traverse and opened fire on the National Guard vehicle from less than ten yards away. The 20 mm rounds didn't so much puncture the vehicle as penetrate it from one side to the other, destroying the front of the Humvee and everyone inside. The M-249 fell silent after one final, futile burst. Still moving, the Escalade slammed into the smoking wreck and pushed it aside, then swerved into a wild U-turn and accelerated away from the battle zone, heading south.

Bolan was on his feet in a flash, running for the last undamaged Humvee. The driver rolled down his window. "What's your plan?"

The soldier leaped into the rear of the Humvee and pulled back the cocking lever of the M-249. "We've got to stop him before he gets back to the factory! He's going to blow it up!"

16

The driver popped the clutch and hit the gas, making the Humvee's tires smoke on the pavement as they took off after the Escalade, shrinking in the distance.

The driver glanced back at Bolan, who was blinking the tears out of his eyes from the stinging wind. "You realize we're chasing a minigun mounted on a truck that's as heavily armored as a tank, right?"

"There's only so many bullets that thing can hold. I'm guessing he blew through most of his ammo back on Main Street."

"You mean when they were laying waste to the heart of town, right?"

Bolan tried not to wince at the comment. "I think you'll have no trouble getting some assistance from the government to rebuild." At the very least they'll want to keep the fact that a commercial-size meth lab funded by a drug cartel had set up shop right in the middle of America, he thought.

The one advantage they had over the vehicle they were chasing was speed. Cresting the hill outside of town, they saw the Escalade laboring up the next small grade. The driver stomped on the gas, making the Humvee surge forward. "Think they've seen us?"

As if answering his question, a brief burst of fire erupted

from the minigun, the bullets chewing up the road and shoulder, sending up large plumes of dust. The driver wrenched the wheel to the right, swerving onto the opposite shoulder before straightening the Humvee. "Guess so."

"Let's see if I can even the odds a bit." Bolan lined up sights of the M-249 with the chain gun and let loose three bursts. At least one of them hit the gun itself, making sparks fly from the housing, but whatever damage it had sustained hadn't seemed to impair the weapon system. It answered back with another burst that chopped the Humvee's right front fender into scrap metal, making the driver swerve so far over that they nearly went into the ditch.

Seeing the weapon system with its barrels canted down to try to hit them gave Bolan an idea. "Closer! Get closer!"

"You want to do *what?*"

"He'll shoot us to pieces back here! Get beside him. The gun can't decline far enough to hit us!"

"And how am I supposed to get us that close in one piece?"

"I'll do my best to keep it off balance. Go, go, go!"

The driver put the pedal to the metal as Bolan squeezed the trigger on the machine gun again, doing everything in his power to keep the muzzle aimed at the cannon. The recoil of the M-249 shook his hands and arms all the way up to his shoulders, but he gritted his teeth and kept the top of the fleeing Escalade in his sights. Bullets bounced off the housing and mechanism of the chain gun, and Bolan was rewarded with a large burst of sparks and spurt of smoke. It spit one last short burst that chewed up the road in front of the Humvee, then stopped all together, the barrels grinding to a halt and smoke rising from the system.

The driver had been doing his part as well, bringing the Humvee alongside the Escalade, the cloud of dust being kicked up by both vehicles obscuring their vision. "Holy shit, you did it! Now how do we stop the rest of it?"

The Escalade driver chose that moment to swerve his heavier vehicle into the squat Humvee's side, grinding against it in a squeal of metal. The Humvee lurched right, then came back just as hard, slamming into the side of the Cadillac, but hardly budging it.

Bolan squinted through the dust, haze and sunlight to see the Cristobal compound appear in the distance. "Don't let them get to the factory!"

"I'm fuckin' trying!" The driver twisted the wheel hard left again, doing his best to force the Escalade off the road. The SUV and its driver resisted all efforts to divert it from its intended course, and pushed back against the Humvee with implacable power.

Bolan had been letting the machine gun cool down from his previous firing, but he finally shoved the barrel as far down as it could go, then let loose at the Caddy's right front wheel. Although it was a run-flat, there was a limit to the amount of abuse it could take, and several bursts of 5.56 mm rounds far exceeded its capability. The tire shredded apart in a shower of rubber, the whole vehicle lurching down as the rim bit into the road in a spray of sparks. The Escalade just kept on rolling forward, turning onto the short driveway leading to the company grounds.

The driver yanked the wheel over in another futile effort to stop the rolling armored vehicle. "Damn it, man, bust a window open or something!"

"Can't find a weak spot!" Bolan aimed and loosed a long burst at the passenger-side window, seeing it star into opaqueness under the impact of the bullets, but not break. "Damn it! Stay on them!"

But the driver of the Escalade went on the offensive again, smashing his vehicle into the side of the Humvee. The two engines strained against each other, but the Humvee was losing, as the Escalade slowly forced it over to the right, aiming it right at a small, cinder-block building.

"Turn, turn right!" Bolan shouted as he ducked into the rear passenger seat. The driver hauled on the wheel, but they were going too fast. The Humvee had just started to angle away from the building when it slammed into the wall with its right fender—the one already weakened from the burst of machine-gun fire—taking the brunt of the impact.

The entire right front quarter crumpled like tinfoil. The engine backfired and died, leaving an eerie silence in Bolan's ears. The impact had thrown him against the back of the front seats, painfully bruising his left shoulder and ribs and banging his head against the frame of the door hard enough to make him see stars for a few moments. When his vision cleared, Bolan raised his head just high enough to see the motionless form of the driver in the front seat. Checking the man's pulse, Bolan found it steady and strong.

"Good thing you wore your seat belt," he muttered as he wrestled the man out of the straps. Beretta in hand, he was able to push open the passenger's back door, and after checking for hostiles, he slipped out and tried to open the driver's door, to no avail—it was wedged shut. The passenger's door was relatively undamaged, so he was able to go in and haul the man out. He dragged him to the far side of the building, away from the Humvee, which didn't seem to be in danger of catching fire or exploding at the moment. Checking the man over for any obvious injuries, Bolan found none. He left him on the ground and went hunting for De Cavallos.

The grounds of the facility were silent, with none of the previous bustle of people at work. De Cavallos must have let his people go, Bolan thought, trying to scan in all directions for shooters while moving toward the big building he had broken into earlier that morning. While he didn't see the Escalade anywhere, it was the logical destination for both of the De Cavallos men.

Bolan reached the main doors without incident, then realized the key-card reader was flashing red. The entrance had been security locked. He jogged back to the Humvee, removed the SAW from its pintle-mount and carried it back to the entryway. Standing about fifteen yards away, he steadied the weapon on his hip and squeezed the trigger.

The long burst of bullets chopped the thick glass into hundreds of tiny pieces. Bolan kept the carnage going, letting the machine gun spray lead death into the main room as well, in case anyone had gotten the bright idea to try to ambush him as he was coming inside. Only when the gun clicked dry did he let up on the trigger.

The entrance to the building was demolished, with no sign that the glass doors had even existed, save for the scattered fragments of glass on the floor. As he watched, a piece of metal framing broke loose from the top and fell to the ground. Bolan tossed the empty, smoking gun aside, drew his Beretta and strode toward the doorway.

Bits of glass crunched beneath his feet with every step. His hearing battered from the slaughter on Main Street, followed by the run-and-gun back to the Cristobal compound, Bolan felt as if he were listening to the world through ears stuffed with cotton. Everything sounded far away, which could be fatal when hearing a safety click off or a shotgun slide rack meant the difference between life and death.

He kept most of his attention focused on the high, L-shaped desk at the back of the big room, which would provide perfect cover for a person waiting in ambush. Normally he could hear someone breathing or shifting his weight from yards away, but all he could sense at this moment was the blood rushing through his ears. He walked farther into the room, watching the desk, the double doors and the foyer that contained the elevator.

Bolan was almost at the desk when he felt more than heard the ping of the elevator signaling a car had just arrived. Glancing over, he saw the arrival light glowing, which meant the doors were moments away from opening. Quickly he threw himself forward into a shoulder roll that took him to the side of the desk farthest from the elevator. Coming up on his feet again, he flattened his back against the dark hardwood and waited for someone to come out.

The doors cycled open and closed, yet Bolan sensed no one else in the room with him. But he was still hesitant to move any farther—if felt like someone was still in or around there—he just had to figure out where.

Steeling himself, Bolan rolled right, behind the desk, his pistol aimed and ready to shoot anyone behind it.

The space was empty. He crawled forward until he was at the inside corner, where the desk made the ninety-degree turn toward the wall. Bolan peeked up at the room, aware that precious seconds were ticking away. For all he knew, De Cavallos could be moments away from resetting the bomb to destroy the building. He saw the elevator light come on again and stood up, realizing that the mechanism had to have been on a timer that cycled it between the floors.

So when the doors opened and Everado De Cavallos emerged carrying a long, sleek, futuristic-looking gun with a thick drum magazine in the middle, Bolan was caught in the open for a second.

Just long enough for Everado to level the gun and open fire.

Bolan fell backward as the heavy panels of the desk buckled and splinted under the impact of the buckshot from the AA-12 automatic shotgun. He sent up a silent thanks to the powers that be that the young man hadn't loaded the weapon with slugs. The thick hardwood of the desk had barely resisted the lead onslaught, but it couldn't take another full-auto beating without being destroyed.

Quickly Bolan scooted backward on the polished marble floor, heading for the far end of the desk. The piece of furniture shook as it was pounded by more double-ought buckshot.

"Pretty macho torturing an unarmed man who you tied up first, aren't you, Cooper!" Everado shouted. "Why don't you try some of that shit now, huh!?" He let loose more rounds, their impact making the end of the desk closest to him fly apart. "Come on out, tough guy!"

Over or around, Bolan thought, trying to figure the best avenue of attack. He peeked out around the corner of the desk, hoping to catch the punk in the middle of reloading. Unfortunately, he didn't see him at all. Where the hell'd he go?

"My father's gonna burn this place to the ground, and gas those cabrons like this place was Dachau, you know? And there's nothing you can do to stop it, puto!"

His ears were ringing even more now, making the kid sound like he was yelling while underwater. Bolan felt more than heard the thump of something hitting the desk. Then he heard a shot, followed by what felt like a footstep, then another shot.

"Show yourself, Cooper!" Everado's voice was on the ragged edge of hysteria. Bolan knew it was due to a combination of excitement at hunting down his tormentor and rage and fear at being held powerless by another man, then being let go to slink back to his father, beaten and weak. In his current condition he was almost more dangerous than if he was in his right mind, likely to shoot at shadows or imagined sounds—or pulverize the desk Bolan happened to be using for cover.

The shots and steps continued as the Mexican got closer, with Bolan tensing to make his move, while switching the fire selector on his Beretta to 3-shot burst. Everado unleashed one more round, and that's when Bolan went for it, turning and pushing away from the weakened desk while shooting so he could put some distance between the kill-crazy maniac and hopefully putting him down once and for all, too.

However, the moment he pushed off the desk, the entire structure, already stressed by the multiple holes shot through it, started to collapse. Everado flailed wildly as he lost his balance and toppled off the desktop as it broke into several large pieces and fell apart. Unfortunately, he fell just as Bolan was shooting at him, the bullets whizzing harmlessly past to hit the far wall dozens of yards away. The automatic shotgun sailed from his grasp as Everado tried to land on his feet, but failed, planting his face on the pile of shattered and broken wood that had once been a magnificent piece of furniture.

For a moment, they just stared at each other, Bolan holding his Beretta, still pointing into the air, Everado with empty hands and wide eyes watching him. The soldier moved first, pointing his pistol at the young man, only to realize the slide was locked back on an empty chamber.

Everado smiled, his eyes flicking to the shotgun a few yards away. His smile disappeared when Bolan ejected the empty magazine and grabbed a fresh one off his belt. He scrambled over the broken wood and dirty floor toward the gun, throwing himself forward in a frantic slide to grab the handle and whip it around—just in time to see the unblinking black muzzle of the Beretta's sound suppressor stare back at him.

But the Mexican punk surprised Bolan again. Everado wasn't trying to shoot his opponent; instead, he threw the autoshotgun at the other man. The weapon sailed through the air and smacked into Bolan's hands, numbing them enough to jar the pistol loose. The gun hit the floor and slid a few feet away. The soldier sat up and was reaching for it when he was hit by a bantamweight freight train of fists and feet.

Someone had taught the kid to box at some point. Bolan had his hands full just blocking the kid's flurry of punches. He tried to bring up a knee, but Everado blocked it with his thigh, all the while trying to turn the older man's face into hamburger. Bolan put some distance between himself and the half-sized scrapper simply by grabbing his shoulders and hurling him off.

His nose and jaw smarting and his ribs aching from where the kid had planted a shoe on it, Bolan got up and faced Everado, who had also sprung to his feet and had his guard up, his shoes shuffling in the dirt. Heaving a weary sigh, Bolan raised his fists and started walking forward. Everado closed the distance, as well, and when he got within range, Bolan hauled off and kicked him right in the crotch with all his strength.

The effect was paralyzing. Everado's expression changed from half-mad wolfish glee to pained agony in a heartbeat, his mouth locked open in a silent scream as he clutched his privates. With his face exposed, Bolan looped a powerful haymaker under his chin that knocked the wannabe thug right off his feet to the floor, instantly out cold.

Bolan took a deep breath, then got to his feet and walked over to his Beretta. Picking it up, he removed the empty magazine and replaced it with a full one—his last, he noted. Then he trudged over to the shotgun, picked it up, ejected the empty drum and walked back to the motionless young man. Poking around on his body, he uncovered a fully loaded drum. Inserting it into the receiver, Bolan charged the gun and headed for the double doors that led to the rest of the complex.

17

Kicking one of the doors open, Bolan sent a 3-round burst from the AA-12 down the hallway. After the thunderous echo of the blast died away, only silence greeted him. He began advancing down the corridor, alert for lights, movement, sound—anything that would tell him where the elder De Cavallos might be and what he was up to.

If I wanted to take out a pharmaceutical company—check that, industrial meth lab—with as big a bang as possible, where would I go? Bolan wondered. The answer came to him quickly: the production room. The only problem was that he didn't know where it was. Shifting the AA-12 to one hand, Bolan dialed Stony Man Farm.

"Go, Striker."

"Bear, I need a schematic of the Cristobal plant's main building. Specifically, I need to know where the production vats are."

"Akira brought up the blueprints about an hour ago. Where are you currently?"

"Past the main entry room, about twenty yards down the long hallway on the left."

"Have you passed the dry chemical storage room yet?"

Bolan checked his position in the hall. "No, it's two doors down."

"Okay, you're close. Proceed ahead approximately fifty yards, past four labs on your left and the storage room, which takes up all of the space to your right. If they followed the plans, the production vats capable of cooking up what looks like about a ton of meth at once will be through the fifth door on your left."

"Thanks, Bear." Bolan cut the call and continued down the hallway, counting off doors as he went. At the fifth one, he realized he could have skipped the call in the first place, since the air lock door was clearly marked: Chemical Compound Production Facilities—All Personnel Must Wear Proper Hazardous Material Protection Equipment Before Entering.

"Damn." At the very least Bolan wanted to find a respirator before going in. No sense trying to kill the guy if you were going to have your lungs turned to goo at the same time. Remembering he'd seen an emergency mask container in the storage area, Bolan backtracked and slipped inside the huge room.

INSIDE THE EVEN larger compound production room, De Cavallos looked up as the faint sound of shotgun blasts reached his ears. He was bent over his jury-rigged detonator, interrupted in the process of attaching it to the main chemical production tank, which had been synthesizing about one thousand pounds of methamphetamine. He had halted the production process earlier that morning, and set up the huge metal vat to capture one of the byproducts of meth manufacture, phosphene gas, an odorless, colorless, highly flammable vapor.

A simple programmed timer would release the gas at the proper time—once De Cavallos and his guard were long gone—then another one would ignite a burner five minutes later. The resulting explosion would take out the factory and lay waste to the surrounding countryside, both in the physical damage it would cause, as well as the chemical contamination. All he needed was a few more minutes to ensure that the system would work as he'd planned, then it would be goodbye Cristobal and goodbye Quincyville.

De Cavallos had his personal security guard, Hector Arciera, with him. Formerly of the Mexican navy's special forces group Fuerzas Especiales, like many of his colleagues at Cristobel, he left the military for the more lucrative pay found in drug running. Currently he was guarding the door while his boss worked. When they both heard the repeated blasts of the automatic shotgun, De Cavallos had smiled. But a minute later, Hector, who was watching the hallway using a remote monitor slaved into the plant's security system, frowned and got his boss's attention.

"Chief, that Cooper guy is coming down the hall...he's talking on a cell phone...he's coming this way."

"Kill that bastard once and for all, will you, but no shooting in here. Hit one of the tanks and we're all dead!"

De Cavallos scooted around until he was behind the main tank, while Hector drew his Gerber double-edged fighting dagger and took a position behind the door, ready to stab the man as he came in. With everything in the room turned off, both men strained their ears to catch the footsteps of the man who had taken just less than twenty-four hours to destroy everything they had worked to build over the past several years.

They waited five seconds...ten...fifteen... But no one came through the air lock.

"Where is he?" De Cavallos hissed.

His bodyguard shrugged. "I don't know. He should have been here by now." He checked the monitor again. "Looks like he's heading for the dry storage room."

"Well, make sure he never comes out."

With a nod, Hector checked the action on his H&K MP-5 and cycled through the air lock, heading down the corridor.

INSIDE THE CAVERNOUS room, Bolan crossed the empty space to the far wall near the door he had entered in earlier that morning. As he'd thought, there was a large yellow box on the wall marked Oxygen Respirators: Use In The Event Of Chemical Contamination.

Popping the box open, he grabbed the full-face mask and small yellow tank, slinging the oxygen supply over his shoulder and perching the mask on top of his head, then turned back toward the door—only to find himself in the sights of a submachine gun aimed by a man he'd never seen before.

The warrior dived to one side, tucking and rolling as the man blasted away at him. At that range, Bolan knew there was only about a fifty percent chance of hitting a moving target with an automatic weapon, even with training. He just had to reach some kind of cover, which he did with one more shoulder roll, skidding behind a large rack of metal shelves several stories high, each level holding pallets of various colored barrels. Hearing footsteps, Bolan didn't stop, but ran down the narrow aisle formed by the high shelves, rounding a corner and running to the next intersection, then turning left again, back toward the rear exit.

He stopped for just a moment to make sure the canister was secure and undamaged, then looked up and began climbing, figuring the best way to get the drop on the guy would be from thirty feet in the air. With one last heave, he pulled himself onto a wooden pallet atop a cluster of green barrels. No sooner had he rolled over than a line of slugs chewed into the wood next to him, spraying him with splinters. Bolan looked up to see the mystery gunman standing on a similar platform twenty yards away, adjusting his aim. He rolled back off the platform, grabbing the edge with one hand but losing his grip on the shotgun, which fell to the floor with a loud clatter.

Bolan heard approaching footsteps shake the shelves as the shooter closed in. Seeing a narrow space between the top level and the full pallet below it, Bolan wriggled inside, pushing himself forward into the darkness. Shrugging off the oxygen tank, he wedged it into a corner, then tucked his legs up, drew his Beretta again and waited. He heard the man's steps on the pallets above his head, listened to them recede and approach as he searched the surrounding area.

Holstering his pistol, Bolan spread his weight out on his hands and feet and slowly crawled to the back of the pallet, where the deep corridor formed by the two tall shelves of chemicals was shadowed in darkness. He waited until he heard the man cross to the far side again, then began climbing up the side of the topmost pallet, trying to move only when he heard the other man move. The strain on his already taxed muscles was terrific, but Bolan kept going, rising inch-by-inch until his head was almost level with the topmost pallet. Securing his feet on the lower pallet, he drew his pistol and peeked over the top.

The gunman stood a few feet away on his right, looking down at the floor where the shotgun had fallen. As Bolan started to bring up his pistol, the man turned and spotted his quarry staring at him from the back side of the shelf unit. He brought his submachine gun around and fired from the hip as Bolan triggered a 3-round burst of his own.

The Executioner's steadiness was the only thing that saved him. The shooter's burst chopped wood right next to him, making Bolan turn his head to prevent taking a sliver in the eye. His rounds hit the man square in the chest, making him sit down close to the edge, but not falling over. Steadying himself, the gunner aimed the MP-5 with one hand and loosed wild burst that made Bolan duck for cover, chips of wood flying over his head.

Damn, he's wearing a vest, Bolan thought. Knowing every minute he was delayed with this gunman was one more minute De Cavallos had to finish sabotaging the plant, Bolan stuck his pistol up and fired several rounds blindly in his opponent's direction. Hearing a startled curse, he figured he might have tagged him, or at least made him take cover as well. A clatter from the other side of the shelving caused Bolan to look down as the roar of subgun fire filled the room. He saw a flash light up the dim space as the gunman tried to hit him by firing through the space between the load and the level above.

Bolan was already scrambling up to try to catch the gunman from behind, but when he got to the top and burst over, pistol in hand, the soldier found the pallet deserted. Rising to his feet, he calmed the blood pounding in his ears and focused on locating his opponent's position. His breath panted out between his teeth, and he was aware of beads of sweat trickling down the back of his neck.

Taking two stealthy steps to the right, Bolan strained to hear any sound that might give away the man's hiding spot. Suddenly wood chips exploded from where he had previously stood as a burst of 9 mm rounds tore across the top of the platform. Bolan returned the favor and sent two 3-round bursts toward where the bullets had come from while stepping away from his previous position. The other man returned fire, raking the top of the platform again. Bolan could tell from the angle of the shots that he was firing from the side up. Figuring the best defense was a good offense, he ran over and was rewarded by seeing the man tucked into the space between two pallets, about to load another magazine into his MP-5.

"Hey." Bolan pointed his pistol down and when the man glanced up instinctively, shot him in the left eye. Relaxing in death, the gunner's body slid out of the crevice and tumbled to the floor.

Holstering his Beretta, Bolan jogged back to the corner of the shelf, retrieved his oxygen mask and canister, and climbed down. Slinging it over his shoulder, he picked up the shotgun, checked its action, then headed for the exit, pausing only to grab the dead man's key card on the way.

Back in the hallway, he put on the mask and made sure the seal around his face was tight, then readied the shotgun and headed for the chemical production room. Swiping the card gained him instant access to the first door. Bolan edged inside, shotgun leading, and waited for the outer door to close before swiping the card through the second reader. The inner door opened, and he stepped inside.

The white, immaculate room wasn't as large as the chemical storage room, but it was impressive nonetheless. Most of the space was taken up with three large vats, at least twenty feet tall, that lined the far side of the room. Beneath one of them lay the signs of planned destruction—a jury-rigged timer that was counting down from four minutes. It was attached to a valve that would vent gas from the first tank—something flammable, no doubt. All it would take was some kind of flame to ignite it, and the whole building would go up. And next to it was a simple Bunsen burner, the kind found in most high schools, that would provide the flame.

Glancing right and left, Bolan started for the timer, intending to tear it right off the mounting. As he approached, a shadow fell over him, and he sensed someone behind him. Before he could turn, he felt agonizing pain course through his entire body, his eyes and hearing and other senses short-circuited by white-hot electricity.

His spine spasming from the jolt, Bolan fell to the floor, the shotgun kicked away from his numb fingers. He reached for it, but was blasted again with another searing jolt of electricity that made him curl up, his arms and legs twitching uselessly. Rolling onto his back, Bolan saw how De Cavallos had gotten the drop on him—the air lock extended *into* the room, giving him a small platform to climb to and jump down from.

"Mr. Cooper, somehow I had a feeling that it would be

you coming through that door, not my man. I assume that you've killed him, along with my son. Therefore it is only fitting that you will die in here, too."

He pressed the stun baton hard into Bolan's chest a third time, the current making him arch his back and grit his teeth as the voltage coursed through him. De Cavallos held it there for several seconds, a thin, feral grin creasing his features.

"As I'd said in town, soon there will be one less hero in America." He reached down and plucked the key card from Bolan's pocket, then reached over and grabbed the shotgun off the floor. "Goodbye, Mr. Cooper." He turned, swiped the card through the reader, then stepped through, smashing the end of the baton into the keypad inside the room. Bolan rolled over again to see him shatter the reader on the other side, then swipe the card through the outer door's reader and leave.

Bolan pushed himself over onto his hands and knees, fighting the urge to throw up. His skin tingled with every movement, as if the shocks were still coursing through his body. Raising his head, he stared at the timer on the vat nozzle through eyes that were still coming into focus. It had just ticked down to under two minutes.

The warrior crawled toward the timer, one torturous foot at a time, hand out in front, then a leg, then another hand, then another leg. His head pounded from the repeated stunning, and there was a bitter, metallic taste in his mouth, but he kept going. He reached the mechanism as the timer counted below one minute. Rearing back on his haunches, Bolan studied the timer attached to the nozzle, tracing the wires, then shrugged. Grabbing them all in one hand, he tore them out with a hard yank. The timer kept counting down, but with no way to send the signal to open the nozzle, he figured he was safe. Just to be sure, he disabled the timer on the burner by smashing it with the butt of his pistol.

The crisis averted, Bolan turned his attention to figuring

out how to get out of the room. A quick pace of the perimeter revealed that the air lock was the only way in or out. The vents were too small, and also blocked by fans. Bolan only had his Beretta, which would be useless against the thick, wire-embedded glass, and the oxygen mask and tank. He considered fashioning some kind of explosive device out of the tank, but quickly rejected the idea, as the concussion in such an enclosed space would probably knock him unconscious, or do even worse damage. He turned to a long lab table covered with beakers, test tubes and pipettes that stood opposite the vats.

Examining the various chemicals, he spotted a large glass beaker with a heavy rubber stopper at one end, filled with a clear liquid. On it was the simple label *Hcl*. Grabbing it, Bolan walked back to the air lock and examined the seal between the glass and the metal frame. When he was satisfied, he shoved a stool over and carefully climbed on, holding the beaker with both hands. He set it on top of the air lock, then climbed atop the platform. Once there, he made sure his mask was secure, then drew his Beretta and put five shots into the glass near the corner. As he'd hoped, the entire pane starred, but didn't break due to the wire holding the layers together.

Removing the stopper, he poured the liquid on the seam between the glass and the metal. The steel began to smoke as the concentrated hydrochloric acid ate through it. Bolan didn't know if he had enough to weaken the entire plate, so he concentrated the acid on two adjoining sides, hoping that would be enough for him to be able to break a hole through the weakened glass large enough to get out.

The fumes rose up as the acid continued corroding the metal, and Bolan felt the heat from the chemical exchange waft over him. He held the mask firmly in place, knowing that breathing in the fumes could cause illness, and long-term exposure would result in death.

A red light flashed on, and a siren blared in the laboratory. Bolan took this as a good sign, figuring he'd most likely breached the air lock. Then he stepped carefully on the edge of the structure, and stomped hard on the corner where he'd poured most of the acid. It buckled, but still held. He stomped on it again, aware that the sole of his boot was smoking from the residual acid on the glass. The corner buckled, and he kept stomping on it until it bent, creating a hole large enough for him to drop through. The only problem was the leftover acid on the glass and metal. Bolan looked around for a lab coat or something to protect himself, but there was nothing immediately available. Tearing the sleeves off his shirt, he wrapped them around his hands, then grabbed the edges of the frame and dropped into the air lock. The next thing he did was to get rid of the cloth, which was already reacting to the acid it had absorbed.

Although the keypad to the outer door was glowing red, indicating the door was locked down, Bolan had encountered enough of them that he knew how to jury-rig a bypass as long as the pad was complete. The hard part was removing the keypad, which he managed to do with his dagger. Running the bypass took another two minutes before Bolan could step out into the empty hallway.

The entire corridor was bathed in red emergency lights, and a recorded woman's voice warned that all personnel should evacuate due to a possible chemical leak. Bolan ran to the large room, where he spotted Everado's motionless body still lying on the floor amid the rubble of the desk. Heartless bastard didn't even check on his own son, he thought as he ran for the main doors and out into the bright morning light. Spotting De Cavallos in the extended Escalade leaving through the front gate, he sprinted around the corner, hoping to find a vehicle in which to give chase.

The only vehicle was a small semi used to move trailers throughout the compound. Bolan glanced around, ran to the corner of the building and spotted a white Mercedes-Benz AMG coupe with a license plate that read DECAV1. He raced toward it.

Busting out the driver's side window with one shot, he was in, and had disabled the alarm and hotwired the car in less than two minutes. Peeling out, he took off after the Escalade.

The sport sedan caught up with the SUV in less than a mile. However, now that Bolan was near him, he had to figure out a way to stop De Cavallos. The car wasn't nearly heavy enough to run the Cadillac off the road, and Bolan had no weapons that would penetrate the armor. He only had the car....

Juking left, the Executioner mashed the gas pedal to the floor, and when De Cavallos swerved to try to cut him off, Bolan cut right and sped past the lumbering SUV to the open road ahead. Shots rang out behind him, but the soldier concentrated on putting as much distance between him and the Escalade as possible. The flat ribbon of highway stretched into the distance, vanishing into the horizon. When Bolan could no longer see the SUV in his rearview mirror, he stomped on the brakes and spun the wheel hard right, sending the luxury automobile into a bootlegger's turn. The car spun 180 degrees and stopped when facing the direction he had just come from. Buckling his seat belt, Bolan drove into the center of the highway, stopped the car and waited.

A few seconds later, the Escalade appeared in the distance. De Cavallos braked when he saw the car idling in the middle of the empty highway. Seconds passed.

Bolan just stared at the motionless Escalade, one hand on the steering wheel, one hand on the gearshift. He imagined he could see the other man behind the wheel of the SUV wondering if Bolan was serious, wondering if he could survive the next few minutes. Wondering if his vehicle would survive the contest—and knowing there was no way out except through the other car.

Bolan simply wondered if the other man had finally figured out that he hardly ever bluffed.

With a squeal of tires and roar of the engine, the Escalade leaped forward, its run-flat tires slapping at the pavement as it gathered speed.

Bolan popped the clutch and laid black rubber on the road as the Mercedes-Benz surged forward, the acceleration pressing him back in his seat.

The two vehicles closed the distance between them rapidly, the tall Escalade quickly filling the sedan's windshield. Bolan set his arms and hung on grimly, aware that he'd have no time to turn in the next two seconds—and not planning to anyway.

The space between them shrank to nothing in a few seconds. Bolan was close enough to see the whites of De Cavallos's eyes, see his hands clutching the steering wheel of the SUV with iron-hard determination. But at the last second—he blinked.

The drug runner hauled the wheel of his truck hard right when the vehicles were less than twenty yards apart. The heavy Escalade started to turn, but Bolan steered with him, sending the sedan into the side of the SUV. With its forward momentum redirected by the collision, the nose of the speeding car plowed into the passenger door of the Escalade hard enough to flip the SUV.

Its front end destroyed, the Mercedes-Benz spun off at its own crazy angle, rising up on its two driver's-side wheels before crashing back down to the ground. The car continuing its spin out until it hit the ditch on the other side of the road, finally coming to a jarring stop half in and half out of the ditch, its crumpled, smoking hood pointing toward the sky.

Surrounded by several rapidly deflating air bags, Bolan

shook his head and checked himself over. As he'd expected, the solid German engineering had enabled him to walk away from the accident with sore muscles, but no permanent or life-threatening injuries.

Pushing open the door, he got out, drew his Beretta and walked over to the Escalade, which had ended up on its roof, the cab crushed under the weight of the vehicle, its rear wheels spinning uselessly. De Cavallos had been thrown from the vehicle during its wild crash, and he lay pinned underneath the bulk of the SUV, his face and arms flushed from the blood forced out of his crushed limbs. Bolan aimed his pistol at the man, but lowered it just as quickly when he realized there was no need for a bullet.

De Cavallos gasped for breath when he saw his tormentor approach. "I couldn't…believe…my eyes…when I saw you…in my car…I never thought…you'd get out…of the lab…."

"I thought you'd have figured out by now I don't give up easily." Bolan knelt by the man. "I wanted to tell you that your son is still alive."

"Everado's…alive?"

"Yeah, and I'm taking him in to testify about everything that's happened here. Between that and what the Bittermans' daughter can tell the police, Cristobal will be shut down faster than you were."

De Cavallos had no answer for that, he just sucked in a weak breath, then let it out again—the last one he'd ever have. Bolan reached down and closed his eyes, then stood and pulled out his cell phone and dialed a number.

"Rollins…yeah, it's done…have someone come pick me up, would you? I'm about five miles out of town. Yeah, they'll find me…I'll be the beat-up guy walking on the side of the road."

He disconnected, then dialed another number. "Bear? Yeah, it's me. It's all over."

Epilogue

"If you'd told me you were answering my call on a hospital gurney, I'd have found another way back to town."

That afternoon, Bolan stood by Rollins's hospital bed. The restaurant owner had his arm in a sling, and a bandage covered the top of his head where he'd taken a nasty cut from a piece of flying shrapnel. The doctor had assured Bolan that the man was going to come out of the battle on Main Street, as the survivors were already calling it, with no permanent injuries.

Rollins reached out his uninjured hand, which Bolan took and pumped firmly. "It was worth it to get our town back. Hell, it would have been worth it if I hadn't made it out of there alive, just knowing that I'd done everything I could for my home and the people I care about."

Bolan just nodded, swallowing around the lump in his throat. After all, the same couldn't be said for everyone who'd been involved in the firefight. Although they'd won the battle, they had taken severe casualties. Eighteen townspeople had been killed, with another thirty-five injured, nine severely. Bolan had spent a good deal of time in the morgue, viewing every body and getting as much data as he could on them so he could get Hal Bronola to arrange for government benefits for their families. While everyone involved had volunteered, it shouldn't have gone down the way it had, and Bolan would carry that scar on his soul for the rest of his life, added to the ones that had already been placed there during his endless war.

"I suppose you'll be heading out, back to wherever you were going before you stumbled on our little town in the middle of nowhere, huh?"

"Yeah, but I'm going to make sure you're able to rebuild, and that everyone involved in the battle and their families are taken care of. Too many of you made the ultimate sacrifice, and I'm not going to forget that."

Rollins nodded. "Thanks, Matt. By the way, just how is this going to be spun to the press, anyway?"

Bolan smiled wearily. "Your intrepid newspaper editor is busy as we speak writing the story that's going to make her career, about a group of heroic townspeople who stood up for what they believed in and took back their town from a large group of Mexican drug runners who had set up a giant meth lab nearby. Faced with the townspeople's demand that they get out of town, the drug runners decided to take their revenge and shoot up the town, leading to a terrible shootout on Main Street."

"But no mention of a lone federal agent who tipped them off to the fact that a drug cartel was camping out in their backyard? If not, I'd expect that a bunch of us are going to face a lot of charges for assault with a deadly weapon, and the like."

Bolan shook his head. "That doesn't make interesting reading. You leave the law to me. Just tell your story, and there's no way the government will come down on a group of townspeople trying to defend their homes against invading criminals. Our country needs homegrown heroes, and I think there are plenty right here. Besides, you just make sure to point those agents to the factory. I think they'll find everything they need for a massive case against the rest of the Cristobal company. That should keep them busy enough so they won't look at what happened here too closely. Also, I'd expect a media storm to descend on Quincyville in the next few days, so you might want to make sure those in the know have their story straight."

"Don't worry. We'll make sure anyone involved will tell it just like it happened."

"That's the spirit. You folks will do just fine. And the next time I'm in the area, I'll be sure to stop by."

"You be sure and come by the diner when you do. Dinner'll be on me."

Bolan smiled, a real one this time. "You're on." He shook Rollins's hand once more and walked out of the room.

"Surely you weren't planning on leaving without saying goodbye?"

He'd heard those words before, but the voice saying them was off somehow. Turning, Bolan saw Kelly Bitterman sitting in a chair near the wall. She'd cleaned up, and looked so much like an All-American teenager it was hard to think about what she'd been through over the past two days.

He walked over and squatted next to her. "Not a chance. Are you going to be all right?"

Kelly shrugged, staring at the floor. "I don't know. So much has happened. I guess I'm still trying to deal with everything. It's like it hasn't hit me yet—my parents dead, killers coming after me, the town nearly destroyed… Looking back on all of it, it's almost like it happened to someone else, and I was only watching." She glanced at him. "But it all really happened, didn't it?"

"Yeah, unfortunately it did. What are you planning on doing now?"

"My grandmother lives in the Pacific Northwest. I'm going to go there, put some distance between myself and here until they call me back to testify." She stared at him. "What about you?"

"I've got to head out before the government folks show up and start asking a whole bunch of questions." He scribbled a phone number on the back of a card and handed it to her. "If you ever need to talk about what happened here, day or night, just call this number, okay?"

"Will you pick up if I do?"

"Maybe. If I can't, I'll get in touch as soon as I get your message." He stood up, and Kelly stood as well, then surprised him by throwing her arms around him and hugging him tightly.

"Thank you, Mr. Cooper."

Bolan hesitated, then put his arms around her.

After a minute, he gently disengaged from her. "You're going to be all right, Kelly—I can tell. You take care of yourself, okay?"

"Okay."

Bolan turned and walked to the elevator. He felt the girl's stare on him as he went, but he didn't look back.

Outside, he walked through the hospital parking lot until he found his rental SUV, got in and pulled out, navigating the town's streets. He avoided Main Street, although he could still catch a whiff of smoke from the battle every so often, and he could see light plumes drifting up from the remains of the fires that were put out earlier that day.

Bolan drove out of town, not pausing until he reached the intersection to the highway. There he stopped, lowered his window and looked at the sign that had brought him to the little town in the first place:

Visit Quincyville
The Best Little Town in the Midwest!

"Maybe it finally can be," he said to himself, raising the window again and turning east onto the highway, driving toward the horizon.

* * * * *

TAKE 'EM FREE

2 action-packed novels plus a mystery bonus

NO RISK

NO OBLIGATION TO BUY

James Axler
Outlanders®

INFESTATION CUBED

**Earth's saviors are on the run as
more nightmares descend upon Earth…**

Ullikummis, the would-be cruel master of Earth, has captured
Brigid Baptiste, luring Kane and Grant on a dangerous pursuit. All
while pan-terrestrial scientists conduct a horrifying experiment
in parasitic mind control. But true evil has yet to reveal itself, as
the alliance scrambles to regroup—before humankind loses its
last and only hope.

Available November wherever books are sold.

AleX Archer
THE ORACLE'S MESSAGE

Men would do anything for it...
but one woman will determine its fate

The Pearl of Palawan is rumored to grant a power long coveted by mankind—immortality. Out of curiosity archaeologist Annja Creed finds herself drawn into a group of German divers looking for the fabled pearl. The race is on but no one realizes the true nature of the artifact, or the danger it poses to them all.

Available September
wherever books are sold.